NOT EASY BEING SONIA
AND OTHER STORIES

NOT EASY BEING SONIA AND OTHER STORIES

BY

SAROJ KULSHRESHTHA

First Published, 2018

Published by

GenNext Publication
5, Ansari Road
Daryaganj, New Delhi-110002
Phone: 9811692060
E-mail: gennextpublication@hotmail.com

Printed at: G. Print Process, Delhi.

Cataloging in Publication Data—DK
Courtesy: D.K. Agencies (P) Ltd. <docinfo@dkagencies.com>

Kulshreshtha, Saroj, author.
Not easy being Sonia and Other Stories / by Saroj Kulshreshtha.
pages cm
Short stories.
Contents: Not easy being Sonia — Kenyi -- Whistle-stop of the sunshine express — Whirlpool — Narayani — Laukhi — Baba's birthday gift — Would she really want to know? — God be her guardian angel — Written in the stars — How could you papa?.
ISBN 9789380223384 (PB)

1. Short stories, Indic (English) I. Title.

LCC PR9499.4.K85N68 2018 | DDC 823.92 23

Contents

Acknowledgement

I express my gratitude to my first guide and inspiration, father, Dr Virendra Verma who served as Principal at the National Defence Academy, Khadakvasla, Pune. He was my sole teacher during college years. We made trips to libraries and he was insistent I made my own notes after consulting several books. This gave a unique flavour to them and helped me get the essence. Keys that flooded the market were not permitted. The well-stocked library at our home was the nursery where the seeds of love for English literature were sown. After retirement he wrote a slew of books for children and war stories and biographies of great men and war heroes. I had the good fortune of doing the proofreading of some of his books.

A special thanks is extended to friends and relatives who shared their experiences with me. These form the backbone of my stories.

I am also thankful to my husband, Dr S. K. Kulshrestha for being supportive in my ventures.

Saroj Kulshreshtha

Preface

Unnerved by a fast-fading memory I decided to do something about it. Learning a new language, a panacea for such a problem, was a bit farfetched. The next best was loads of reading and writing. So, at the age of 63 I enrolled for the Creative English Writing course of IGNOU. The paucity of libraries in the neighbourhood took me to the Net. The treasure trove of short stories took me by surprise. I read the old masters and for the first time got acquainted with new trends in story- telling, especially from the Latin American world.

Reading great work is wonderful but for writing one has to draw upon one's own experiences and word power. The simple language and choice of characters will, I hope, touch the inner cord in my readers. My stories are peopled with men, women and children going through their humdrum lives with fortitude, dignity and family support. We may see our own follies and predicaments in them.

The lead story, *Not easy being Sonia*, is my favourite. The feminist in me makes me proud of the way Sonia conducts herself and lives life on her own terms. A lot of people, especially women, will snigger at her, "Look at this foolish woman! She had it all and threw it away. Too much education and independence can addle one's brain!"

Kenyi and *Whistle-stop of the sunshine express* are about two children. Kenyi is the hub of her devoted family but the smart little fellow in the latter story is unable to live up to his full potential for lack of filial support.

Whirlpool, Narayani, Laukhi, Would she really want to know, and *God be her guardian angel* are all women-centric but about very different personalities. All have to find solutions that suit them best and move on in life.

Baba's birthday gift shows how fast times and people are changing.

Written in the stars is the only fun story.

The last story, *How could you papa?,* is the result of the horror tales of rape and murder. It came to my mind that it is not just the victim and her family who suffer but also the family of the rapist. The feeling of shame and horror is different but the intensity of suffering is the same.

Saroj Kulshreshtha

1

Not easy being Sonia

Am I a traditional Indian Housewife or am I an emancipated, educated, freethinking woman of courage who will brook no injustice? I do not know. When our psychology lecturer at the Central Institute of Education, Delhi, gave us too many meaningless questionnaires to fill I confronted her. My brief was," You ask us how we will react under given circumstances. The situations presented are ideal. We, as intelligent people will naturally tick mark what we *should* do under those ideal situations. That does not necessarily mean we *will* act that way when faced with a real life situation. That rubbishes the data collected as it will give wrong information." I do not know what she thought of it but we stopped getting further inane questionnaires.

Thus it is with life. In an effort to be just (and this has been an obsession since childhood) I try to delve deep into the factors that have made Sonia what she is and am amazed at what I find. I fight for justice but would I have fought for myself if I had been unfairly treated? It is easy to succumb to a life of ease and let life roll by, much like sitting on the beach and exulting as the waves come in and gently lap at one's feet. A tsunami? That would be different. Faced with constant emotional trauma, would I meekly seek comfort in age-old recipes or would I fight and live life on my own terms? Only one thing I am sure of—it is not easy being Sonia!

She is new to the colony but so are we all. What's different is that she is a divorcee. A short letter in the mail reveals what could well have been left untold. Her father requests that as his daughter is going through a traumatic period in her life, she be treated with gentleness. He, for good measure, assures that his daughter is no man-eater and all she needs is a home she can visit once in a while!

This sends danger bells trilling. There are friends and then there are *friends*. Some are addressed as 'Mrs.'... Those younger are called by their names. Over the years, a sense of familiarity and affection results in Mrs... being called by her first name. How does one address a divorcee, more or less one's own age, and a very fresh acquaintance at that? 'Mrs.' somehow seems inappropriate as the man the surname belongs to is history. So, everyone calls her Sonia.

There is not much that is nice said about Sonia. Whatever the father may have written, this fashionably dressed forty-plus woman likes men. Her pretensions to feminism fly out the window when, for each debatable issue, she looks for answers not from her gender but from 'the more knowledgeable', and presumably more intelligent, men folk! This, naturally does nothing to endear her to the woman she is out to befriend. Even as the hostess busies herself with preparing tea, Sonia casts sidelong glances in the direction of the husband, who poor thing, knowing which side his bread is buttered and, more importantly, who is going to prepare the next meal, keeps out of the way and busies himself in the study.

Youngsters laugh behind her back as she likes to show how young she is. Girls a few years older than her daughter are her friends but other people's children may not call her 'Aunty'! Unfortunately, the latter do not see in her a kindred spirit 'more or less their own age' sharing their interests and concerns. Children follow her chanting, "Aunty, Aunty!" They scuttle off when she turns to confront them. Her assumed USP is her undoing. The keen interest and understanding of any and every subject to win attention of young men puts off their wives and girlfriends.

Sudha complains," You were right Aunty, until now she was trying to impress Uncle but when he left the room, she is out to seduce the nephew!"

"You are as qualified as she is. Just speak in English and she will know her place!" advises her aunt.

Sonia's was a 'love marriage' and the roller coaster ride of more than a decade had its sweet moments. These gnaw at Sonia's heart from time to time. Attempts to patch up went on and on until one day she realised it was a lost cause. A few months after her entry to the colony, the relationship ended in divorce.

Soon enough, the man married again sending Sonia into a fresh bout of depression. He might have been thrown out from her life but Vineet was a permanent fixture in her talk. After the divorce it was, "I have done him out of a fortune. I made sure he paid a heavy alimony." Now after his second marriage, it is, "He doesn't know what he is letting himself in for. She will keep him under her thumb. She too is an MBA and holds a high post. Soon, you'll see she will leave him." At times, the pain came back and she used the time-honoured tactics to fight it. "What has she got? A hand me down!"

Vineet's second marriage not only lasted, it went on to produce two children. Now Sonia was scared for her own daughter, Bipasha. Would the other woman snatch her child's love too just as she had Vineet's? Shobha, the other woman, made no such move even though she and Vineet assured Bipasha she was more than welcome as the first daughter of the house. Sonia saw designs in this but was proved wrong. Maybe the fault really lay with her.

Most love stories begin and end with the affair culminating in marriage. Love just happens. With lack of nurturing it just withers away. The sheet of paper is there; the story has to be written; it has to be lived. The rose-tinted glasses, unfortunately, get misplaced. He metamorphoses into an oppressive, unfeeling mama's boy and she into a lazy, ever-complaining, selfish nag. All that glittered definitely was not gold. The test by fire proved its baseness. Most of what was taken for love was an act put on to charm a potential spouse. The fun is in the sense of achievement. It proves your worth. That done, the fervour cools down. Most lovers are in love with love, not the person.

Sonia is an American Indian. A big problem with cross-culture marriages such as Sonia's is that the very qualities that attracted the boy and the girl to each other in the first place later seem shallow or unimportant. The nimble-footed young girl with the cherubic smile was the soul of your peer group parties but she definitely does not fit into the joint family. The rose tinted-glasses are substituted with a magnifying glass. Each shortcoming gets enlarged and with horror they realise they've made a mistake. Unfortunately, it is too late. If at the dating stage their parents had pointed out the differences in values and upbringing the couple in love would have taken up the cudgels for each other. Now the cudgels are against each other. I guess each has to make his or her share of mistakes. Unfortunately, the learning process is highly corrosive and soon there is no relationship left worth striving for. Something gives and a divorce follows.

So it was with Sonia and Vineet. They had loved with blinkers on. When the cultural differences made their demands, love showed its wear and tear. Brought up in a western atmosphere where her mother's mother was family and father's relatives rarely visited, she thought that was the natural and correct thing. The Hindu family with in-laws putting in an appearance every now and then was beyond her ken. She considered her husband's family uneducated and that equated them with being uncultured as well. "All the women can talk about is sarees and jewellery. All are dumb housewives with no ambitions of their own!"she sneered.

What is culture? Sonia and Vineet had major differences on this. Sonia was of the firm opinion that in-laws should be outlawed. She hated the word *'Bahu'* which to her was a synonym for bonded slavery. Not to say she ever did or was expected to do work at her in-laws' place. It was a huge feudal set-up with servants crawling all over the place more than eager to please the new bride and get *baksheesh* in return. Sonia hated their fawning ways. Besides, she was used to doing her own work! As a matter of fact she hated a lot of things. Her husband was the baby of his house and loved his family very much. She hated this most. As was their tradition, they wanted to shower gifts on her. This made her uneasy. It was not the done thing at her father's. On his part, Vineet considered refusal of gifts from the elders as show of disrespect and disaffection. This to him was a gross misdemeanor.

Vineet's new posting at Baroda was like a dream fulfilled. Sonia could, at last, do things her way. She was enjoying her newfound freedom when her mother in-law decided to pay a visit. Sonia resented the extra workload. She also resented having to play the ideal *bahu,* that too in her own home. Getting up early, cooking a variety of Gujarati dishes; picking flowers for the *puja* and sitting by her mother-in-law and making small talk was too much for her. She complained to her mother that she was even expected to eat food only after her husband had had his. The mother fumed, "This is boorish!" Vineet saw nothing extraordinary in this. All his colleagues' wives did that. However, he helpfully suggested she nibble on an apple and a large wedge of her favorite chocolate cake while she waited. That did it. "I'm not a fraud like your dear Sarla bhabhi," fumed Sonia, "the moment Prakash leaves home she fries a mound of pakoras to eat while she watches those stupid saas bahu serials!"

"What is wrong with that if it makes her happy? She is expecting and needs the extra nourishment!"

It goes to Sonia's credit that she did learn to speak and write Gujarati so she could communicate with her mother-in-law. Maybe it would have made a better impression had she not constantly reminded all and sundry of this great favour she had done her in-laws.

Sonia became pregnant. The in-laws were jubilant. Her parents said, "You should have waited, where was the hurry?" The custom was that the first child be delivered at the woman's parental home. Sonia too would have been more comfortable with that but her mother would have none of this so there was no option but to have the baby at Ahmedabad. A baby girl was born and became the nucleus of the family. However, Sonia went into postpartum depression. This was a very western thing and nobody could understand it. It didn't make matters easy that Sonia rarely had the baby to herself. She thought it was a deliberate act to alienate the little one from her. She had never been in a joint family otherwise she would have seen it was natural. She might have even enjoyed the leisure time this gave her. The baby was comfortable with all the love and attention she got. She was the darling of the family.

Worse was yet to come. Vineet suffered a stroke. Sonia's parents were alarmed. "Do that computer course you were telling us about before you became pregnant," they urged Sonia, "you will at least be able to stand on your feet should the man pop off!"

Vineet's family was horrified when they heard that instead of being by her husband in his hour of need, Sonia had a more pragmatic agenda. So the baby and Vineet became the responsibility of her in-laws. They, on their part were more than happy to have the two. This is where the family comes in when a member is unwell or in need. They did, however, think it strange that Sonia should think otherwise. Sonia would later complain she had been deprived of the enjoyment of seeing her baby grow. She was not grateful that in her hour of need, when her own family had not helped, her in-laws had not only looked after the baby but done it with love. Come to look at it, this did indeed build a bond between the baby and its father's family and when the child grew older she thought her mother had been selfish and there was a gap which took time to bridge.

Sonia's parents had not only maintained a studied distance from Vineet after the stroke, but had even advised their daughter to do the same. "Do you want to spend the rest of your life nursing a cripple?" they asked. The result was that Sonia's visits to Vineet became few and far between.

With all the tender care his family showered on him, Vineet soon recovered. He had seen through the charade of love and realised Sonia had different priorities. There was no point in continuing with the relationship and soon he and Sonia were divorced. Her parents thought she should have been taken the decision much earlier.

Most people thought something must be wrong with Sonia to give up a rich family and a husband she had once loved. "She should have made more effort," they said. Those who knew Vineet's family said she was lucky to have them as in-laws. They had a social status and were nice people. Guess it was a cultural gap. Neither understood nor tried to understand the other's values. Their minds were set. Marriage is coming to a compromise on tenuous issues but this couple thought they would be compromising their positions by budging an inch.

Sonia's position in people's minds was further weakened by what she uttered thoughtlessly. The more she tried to vilify Vineet, the more they glared at Sonia.

"She has called it on herself!"

"She is always flaunting her high education. Most of us are as well educated."

"What is education anyway if it does not give one the wisdom to face life full on?"

I too thought like the others. I admired her spunk, though. She took up whatever job came her way. She had trained in computers and done a bit of teaching. Vineet had not liked her taking up a job. She was his responsibility he felt. She, on the other hand, wanted to feel useful. After all she had a degree.

Now after so many years spent at home, she felt a bit rusty and besides, the age factor was against her. The jobs she got now were not permanent positions but they did keep her gainfully occupied and helped in keeping off depression and loneliness.

It took me some time to understand that just as giving dowry was taboo for her parents, receiving any gift from relatives was unacceptable to Sonia. She felt she was fleecing them as she was in no position to reciprocate. In our culture, give and take is a part of building bonds. They are not burdens but joyful expressions of love unless, of course, there are demands of dowry. In India, love is given automatically once a relationship is formalised. A daughter-in-law gets love simply because she is the son's wife. We take our duties very seriously. Emphasis on rights, especially individual rights, is a western concept. Even our scriptures tell us to do our duty without expectation of reward. That, hopefully, will come in due course! In Sonia's eyes actions such as touching the feet of elders was specially designed to degrade the *bahu*. Waiting to eat with the husband was not an act of love but a mode of torture. If grandparents loved the child they had ulterior motives. She was paranoid because the child was the only thing she had to call her own and she was scared to lose it to her husband or in-laws. To be fair to Vineet, he had not asked for custody of the child much as his people loved her. He knew Sonia needed her more.

Strangely, in rare moments of enlightenment, Sonia did see a lot of merit in the Indian culture and even poked fun at some western customs but on the whole most times she forgot that her father's side was Indian and she was the recipient as well as ambassador of the two cultures. Disrespect for everything Indian earned derision not respect. People laughed at her as they thought she was putting on airs. She had managed her life badly how then could she go about scattering pearls of wisdom! "Having lived her whole life in this country she still speaks every Indian language like a foreigner," they mocked.

Sonia is still in love with Vineet but he has moved on and now she has accepted it. Initially her talk was so centered round him that though we had never met him we knew all about him, his virtues and vices, mostly the latter. She made attempts to get him back even after he had married again. Wisely he resisted her charms.

If there is a mother-in-law around, Sonia thinks it her bounden duty to put herself in the daughter-in-law's camp. As she constantly impinges herself on the hospitality of the older woman that is hardly sensible! Sonia has an aversion to '*behanjees*'. These unfashionable simple housewives are some sub-human species devoid of learning and culture. Yet when she needs a shoulder to cry on, a cup of hot tea or advice on crucial matters these are the women she goes to. Naturally they feel used and resent it.

Sonia has managed her financial affairs well and also looks after the maintenance of her house efficiently. She has street smartness and is able to deal with all sorts of people. I guess that is one reason I am impressed with her. More than that, she is living a life she enjoys. She has taken up painting lessons to nurture the hobby she had neglected. She has made her daughter, Bipasha, her primary concern and the latter, having a child of her own now, has come to realise what her mother went through and what she did for her. Old animosity has vanished and a new closeness is visible.

Most women would prefer an easy laid-back life in which the husband earned and they kept house. I've seen it even in cases where the husband was unfaithful and the wife knew about it but made her peace. Life outside is too stressful!

It's not easy being Sonia

2

Kenyi

My friend Rupali and her husband Anand had not wanted a child before the end of the fifth year of their marriage but Rupali conceived just at the start of the fifth year. I advised her that since the gift was already on its way, they should accept it gracefully. Hot on the heels of the news of Rupali's pregnancy came news of Anand getting a job in Kenya. All four of us were delighted. Jokingly I said, "If the baby is a boy we can call him Kenyatta and if it's a girl we will call her Kenyi."

In October a lovely baby girl was born. She was named Durga but for me she was Kenyi. The name stuck. For two years I received lovely snaps of her in various stages of development Kenyi in a pram, a pushchair, crawling, taking a tottering step and cutting her first tooth. I got doodles supposedly conveying love for a beloved aunt she had never set eyes upon. I was informed when she said 'Baba' and 'Ma'. "You should see Kenyi dance when Madhuri comes on screen!" wrote Rupali.

Kenyi was about two and a half when communication suddenly stopped and there was deafening silence. I sensed something was not quite right but there was no way of knowing what the matter was. Stray rumours got to me but I thought this could not be my Kenyi. These people were either mistaken or misinformed.

Soon after, we too went away to Nigeria. After twelve long years there we came back home and in an old diary I came across Anand's very first address in Kenya. It was New Year time. Hope filled my heart and I posted a greeting card at that address.

A miracle! I got two long letters from Anand and Rupali. They had been to several countries since that first posting and come full circle. As a matter of fact they were about to leave Kenya again just when my card reached them. The tenuous threads of communication had been revived at last.

The news however was not good. Just as Kenyi turned two, my friend conceived her second child and decided to have her baby at her mother's place in Assam. She thought her babies would be better looked after back home than in Kenya. Shortly before the baby's birth Kenyi came down with fever. She felt hot to the grandmother's touch, very hot but no one worried too much. Viral fever is common in these parts during the early rainy season. Soon after, she started to shake uncontrollably. Anand knew what harm convulsions could do and, ignoring old grandmother tales, he sat Kenyi in a tub of cold water and sponged her until the convulsions stopped and the fever subsided somewhat.

Soon however the fever returned and Kenyi seemed terribly distressed. Her body was badly contorted. Anand held her close and tried to soothe her but she seemed listless almost as if she were in a stupor. The family physician seemed very worried. He suspected it was Japanese Encephalitis and, now that it seemed to have set in, Kenyi would be lucky to come through without terrible damage to the brain.

A virus transmitted by a mosquito causes the disease. It affects the brain that gets inflamed and, if medication does not work, there can be an abscess of the brain which can lead to paralysis or coma.

It was a time of great suffering for the whole family. Anand saw his little darling wilt in his arms. For Rupali it was sheer agony. She had to keep away from Kenyi lest she fall prey herself and pass on the disease to the newborn. This, it later turned out, was erroneous, as this disease is not transmitted by touch. The grandmother kept cursing herself, "If I had not called her home for the delivery, maybe, this would not have happened."

No one was to blame. The child was little and had no immunity to the disease, coming as she did from foreign lands. The combination of season, rural setting, fields of paddy all around had turned the hordes of virus-affected mosquitoes into an army of potential carriers.

Kenyi's condition worsened, her neck was beginning to stiffen. This was a bad sign. She could be severely paralysed or neurologically retarded.

The worst thing about the disease is that it has no cure, not even now, two decades after Kenyi became its victim. There is a preventive vaccine and NRI families visiting areas where the disease is endemic are advised to take it. However, it has its own dangers and anyway Anand did not know of it. He had come home and the thought for viruses lying in wait to attack his little baby never entered his mind. Maybe it was destined to happen. If Rupali had been infected, it would have resulted in an aborted foetus apart from other complications to herself. God had chosen Kenyi.

Intensive supportive therapy was begun in real earnest. Anand's timely hydrotherapy had saved the child from severe brain damage but the working of all organs had to be constantly monitored. Blood pressure and temperature had to be frequently taken. Incubation period is five to fifteen days. Speedy progress of the infection had to be kept under check. That would give time to enable the body to generate anti-bodies to fight the malady. Anti-bodies too take about 15 days to become effective. She was given antibiotics to fight the severe infection. Complete recovery was well neigh impossible. The effort was to contain the damage and ensure that all the vital organs were working to the end of the critical period. Twice during the period Kenyi had seizures and had to be put on intravenous fluids. The respirator was kept on the ready but luckily she did not need it.

When the time of reckoning came, Anand and Rupali realised that tending to Kenyi was going to be a lifelong undertaking. It was the end of their dreams for their first-born. The child had turned into a vegetable. She was no more the bubbly, intelligent charmer. Totally dependent on her parents, she could not be left under anyone else's care. She had to take precedence over the newborn infant, Laxmi, who was left in the care of her grandmother once the weaning was over. It was not easy parting with a babe who could barely recognise them but it had to be done.

For Anand and Rupali the world now became an atlas with circles around cities that had doctors who could help their darling. The slightest glimmer of hope took them scurrying across the globe. Jobs were taken up to be close to doctors heard to perform miracles. Money had to be spent. Money had to be earned. The baby had to be taken to physiotherapists and speech clinics. She had to be massaged and exercised cleaned and fed. She had to be kept amused. It was an uphill task but in the end it brought rewards, maybe very limited, but satisfying nonetheless.

Gradually recognition of her parents lit up Kenyi's wan eyes. The struggle continued. Life returned to her limp limbs and the rag doll could, at last, somehow stand up with help. Daily massages made her legs stronger and then came the day when she took a few ungainly, tottering steps. Some catwalk this! Her parents were over the moon. The first steps she had taken as a baby had filled them with joy but this was extraordinary. This was an answer to their prayers. They were grateful to God for the kindness. New hope kindled their hearts.

Meanwhile, bereft of her parents' love and care Laxmi was growing up too. Anand and Rupali could not enjoy each precious moment of her infancy as they had with Kenyi but they tried to visit India from time to time to see the little one. Laxmi was totally disinterested in Kenyi. What use was a sister who she could not play with? Moreover, as she grew older Laxmi realised she was staying with Grandmother because Mummy and Papa were too busy looking after Kenyi. Her mind was made up, nobody loved her or needed her. She developed a deep-rooted apathy for her entire family. She was what Kenyi might have been had fate not intervened—pretty, smart and intelligent but she lacked Kenyi's warmth.

Kenyi could still not talk. She did utter certain noises that her parents alone could interpret, probably because they knew her every need. Speech therapists could do no more.

Meanwhile, Rupali had a third child. They named her Saraswati completing the trilogy. As little more could be done for Kenyi, there was no problem with her. Indeed, she spread cheer and her laughter kept even Kenyi amused.

Anand thought bringing Laxmi to stay with them might repair the relations with their second daughter. Problem was Laxmi never was able to forgive them. She made no effort to adjust to her family. She groaned, moaned and complained about everything especially about Kenyi. This was unfair as Kenyi's eyes always lit up on the rare occasion Laxmi came into her room. She wanted to play with her just as Saraswati played with her. Laxmi, unlike Saraswati, was horrified at the thought of even being seen with her retarded sister. Indeed she told nobody about her at school. She said she had but one sister, Saraswati.

After Laxmi had completed school, Rupali decided, as she was so bright, it would be best if she stayed at a hostel for further studies. They wanted to fulfil their dreams through her, I guess, and why not? She was brilliant. She went on to medical college, married a classmate and settled down in Siliguri. She rarely asked after her elder sister or visited her parents in Guwahati where they had taken up permanent residence and built a lovely house.

A few years after our return to India, my husband was going on a business trip to the North East. I accompanied him so that we could look in on our friends and their daughters.

I asked for the girls. Anand wryly replied that Laxmi would have nothing to do with the family and Saraswati was doing MBA at Pune.

"Kenyi!" Rupali called out and a shy and innocent-faced young girl walked clumsily into the room. Kenyi is distrustful of strangers and is very choosy about whom she will bestow her favours on. I was delighted that she not only sat beside me but even let me hold her hand. One could see that she was the hub round which the family revolved. Her smile brought sunshine to their faces. A grimace and the whole family were beside her. Tins around the house were full of Kenyi's favourite savories. She does not like sweets and can just about eat rice and dal with a spoon. But snacks are no problem. These she can handle deftly.

All the medicines have made Kenyi obese and all the worries and caring have turned her never-fat parents into shadows of their former selves. Kenyi is taken out for a walk daily and all the people in the neighbourhood know her and she smiles at everybody who looks her way. Anand walks beside her proudly. Together they have achieved the impossible! Kenyi too loves to go on these walks with her father. She shows her pleasure in little chortles accompanied by vigorous slapping of her thighs. Kenyi is fond of music. She loves watching TV and can indicate when she wants the tape recorder to be switched on. Best of all she loves her mother's soft humming. Mummy, she knows, can croon away her pains and sadness. I asked Rupali, "Can you sing?" Her answer was a revelation. "All mothers can sing for their child!" That's true.

One day Anand and Rupali took us to see a new tourist spot that was making waves. It would be tiring for Kenyi so she was left at home with grandmother. For Rupali it was a return to old times. Her childlike laughter still rings in my ear. We took longer than expected. Kenyi's siesta was over and she could not see her mother anywhere. This was unusual. Where was she? When we got home Kenyi and grandmother were sitting on the steps at the entrance. Kenyi was in a foul mood and turned away when her mother handed her the packet of chips she had brought. It was some time before truce was declared.

A couple of months later, Anand visited us. Saraswati was with him. As we busied ourselves in the kitchen, I asked her what her plans for marriage were. I had been asked by Rupali to probe her mind. Anand and

Rupali thought along different lines. Rupali wanted Saraswati to marry and settle down. Anand on the other hand was more concerned about Kenyi's future and thought Saraswati might marry and move away like Laxmi then who would look after Kenyi when he and Rupali were no more. I tried to reason with him that two were better than one and Kenyi would be better off with a married sister and her husband to look after her. Anand was unconvinced. Not only that, he had so brainwashed his youngest daughter that she would listen to nothing said on this subject.

As we sat over a cup of coffee, the talk turned to Kenyi. Anand began, "You are familiar with the circumstances of Kenyi's birth."I opened my mouth to say something but nodded instead. The next words gave me an insight to the soul of the man. "Well," continued Kenyi's father, "I believe she is a goddess sent to take upon herself our pain and suffering! The viral could have affected Rupali or me but it was Kenyi. We didn't name her Durga for nothing. She is *Shakti*, the power that keeps the family going."

And I had been thinking he was referring to that dilemma whether or not to abort the child that had come too early. Suddenly I was ashamed to have even allowed such a presumption to enter my head. Anand rose to a new stature and I was transported to the walks in Guwahati's green glades where Kenyi squealed in delight and slapped her thighs in sheer ecstasy.

3

Whistle-stop of the sunshine express

It is sad not to have children but it's much worse not to be able to love them. My husband and I have been very lucky in this respect. We were on top of the list of favourites among the kids of friends and relatives. The darkness in our lives is immediately dispelled by the smiles that lights up their faces. Our long stay of twelve years in Nigeria became memorable just because we had children around us to love and be loved by. We had a special sendoff exclusively organised by children when we decided to come back home to India. Each presented me with a handkerchief, embroidered ones by girls, painted ones by the boys. Reshma baked her first unaided cake. It was yummy. At the airport I kept feeling they were calling out to me long after they were out of sight.

When we settled down in Delhi I missed the children a lot. Each time neighbours' children called out "Auntie" I thought it was me they were calling out to and almost responded. That was when I decided that I was not going to build any new bonds. Parting is too painful. I immersed myself in my work and the many hobbies I have.

There was a fete in the colony and also an exhibition-cum-sale of paintings and handicrafts. I too put up some paintings. As I mingled with the others appreciating the beautiful things my eyes kept riveting to a bubbly waif of a child looking on wistfully. On an impulse I asked him if he wanted to learn painting. The boy nodded vigorously. He was thrilled. So was his mother.

A couple of days later I was brought to the door by a persistent ringing of the doorbell. The boy was standing there. In gestures, accompanied by noises, he made it known that his mother would be coming in a little while. Obviously, he had been too excited to wait while she got ready!

It was only then I realised that the boy had speech problems!

How did I come to know that the mother would soon follow? The boy had conveyed it all in sign language! I felt quite inadequate for the coming challenge but the exuberance of the boy kept me from backing out. Only on rare occasions had I seen him playing with the other kids. Now I knew the reason. I also realised how much the new venture meant to him. For him, it was something to enjoy and treasure. Something special that he would do exclusively!

I hoped he could at least hear. I decided to use the time to get acquainted. I gave him a sheet of paper and asked him to write his name and age. In neat letters he inscribed "Ravi", 12 years. I was amazed, as he seemed a lot younger with his innocent little face and frail form. I have loads of books from the old days when some of the kids called me "Book Auntie". I got out the Lady Bird series. As soon as Ravi spotted a rose in one of the books he gave himself a neat little slap. This would have surprised me but I had heard the story that someone had plucked the first rose from Mrs. Reddy's rose bush while her son looked on calmly. For that his mother had given him a tight slap. So that little boy was Ravi! No matter if he couldn't speak, this boy had a healthy mind and a sharp memory! It would not be too difficult to communicate with him.

The mother arrived shortly and asked me if I could lend a hand with Ravi's studies in addition to teaching him drawing. He studied at a special school but was not making much progress. In plain-speak, he did not like studies. He would come at four in the evening for an hour each day. I agreed.

The story of Ravi's birth was a sad one. His mother had Rubella during pregnancy. The child was severely affected. Soon it became clear that both his eyesight and hearing were poor. The boy's father who had been delighted at the birth of a boy now lost interest in the child. With the years the relationship got worse. When he came to know the child would never speak properly, he developed an unreasonable apathy verging on hatred towards Ravi. His first born, and a son at that, for him was cause for shame not delight. He made sure no one saw him in the company of his son. What was the child's fault? Mr. Reddy didn't want to delve into such inanities!

Ravi was five when his brother was born. Ravi now became a non-entity. He was put in a school for special children. Scared of his father, he kept as distant from him as he could and confined himself to the shadows of his room from the safety of which he watched his father shower love on the little one. Ravi saw how a tiny silver bell was tinkled near his brother's ear and saw the look of satisfaction on his father's face as the baby gurgled. One day he decided to get to the root of the mystery. He tinkled the bell near his own ear and the strange sound surprised him. He liked the soft sound and tinkled it louder and louder. Yes, it definitely was a pleasant sound. He took it to his brother's ear and jangled it merrily wanting him to share his joy. The sound was much too loud for the baby and he began to howl. The father rushed into the room and caught the culprit red-handed. He laid Ravi across his lap and gave him a sound spanking. His wife pulled Ravi away quickly. He was weeping. Later his Mummy gently told him through gestures not to ring the bell too hard near the baby. Ravi couldn't understand why except that it would earn him a spanking.

Mrs Reddy told me she tried very hard to change her husband's attitude towards Ravi but to no avail.

As the years went by, Ravi found he had nobody to play with. The other children of the colony played cricket. Not Ravi. Not even his brother bothered with him. I have observed that when special children are treated with love and affection in their own homes, outsiders too treat them well. Some such children are the soul of their colonies.

Thus it was that the Sunshine Express whistled into my run-of-the-mill life. The next day, Ravi came around four o'clock. It was teatime and I decided to use teabags to add a little pep. Dip dip went the teabag to the accompaniment of little squeals of delight from Ravi. The boy sure had the ability to turn everything into a celebration of life. Beautiful things had a special appeal and often his thumb and index finger would come together in a gesture of approval. Having received little love from his father, he was deeply touched by even tiny gestures of affection from older men. Right at the outset I had co-opted my husband's collaboration in this venture. I was right. The boy cherished the comments on his work. One day my husband wrote "V. Good" when all the sums were correct. Ravi was ecstatic and henceforth went about signing things off similarly irrespective of their merit! To him, the man with moustaches, my husband, was a very fine fellow, indeed!

In the beginning, things were tough as Ravi was set in the ways of his school. He had learnt everything by heart and liked to go over only what he had already learnt and jot it down in the same order. That I thought was a waste of time. Besides, I wanted him to think for himself. Using counters and coins I ultimately taught him the basics of arithmetic. We played shop with each item's price put on labels we made together and used money in all denominations. I think he enjoyed it and learnt from it. We used all sorts of things from around the house.

I made a cardboard clock with needles that could be moved and soon Ravi was able to tell the time. We also did all sorts of exercises in matching and fill-in-the blanks. I changed the order of questions in the exercises given in his schoolbook. Soon he realised that a trick had been played on him and would study the question before answering. The next logical step was changing a word here and there. Ravi had learnt to think for himself!

Ravi had a good hand and eye. Each day after the first half hour we made something pretty out of scrap lying around the house. Pictures were made using old cardboard, twigs, dry flowers and leaves and bits of cloth and paper. One day we were working on a landscape with a tree, and a hut surrounded with shrubs. I had given him a twig to use as a tree trunk. When it came to the grass, Ravi brought fresh mown grass and for the shrubs he brought the clippings from Thuja bushes. Together we made a tiny tortoise from half a walnut shell and a Humpty Dumpty from an eggshell. The stitches on the rolled out arms and legs of the latter were unbelievably neat. We sat him on a wall made out of empty matchboxes.

Ravi loved doing landscapes. His pictures always had add-ons of flying birds and butterflies. The Sun, the Moon and a sprinkling of stars coexisted. After some time, I stopped pointing to the anomaly.

The books I have are full of pictures. Ravi liked to copy from there. His favourites were little curly haired princesses with billowing skirts. He was charmed by the story of Snow White and the Seven Dwarfs. The day I showed him Walt Disney's cartoon version of the story, he was so thrilled that he kept jumping up and down, chortling.

While Ravi was good at landscapes he took a while learning to draw houses. He had no knowledge of perspective and I had to show him how things appeared smaller when far away. This was not difficult as we mostly sat on the balcony.

Winter was upon us and nice juicy carrots flooded the market. We took the top half of two of the largest, scooped out the inner mass and filled them with water. These we hung up in a window. Soon leaves started to appear and there were two lovely hanging baskets.

As we sat in the sun on the balcony, birds would come and feed on the crumbs put out for them. Ravi looked on fascinated. One day he saw the picture of a parrot in a chart and wanted to copy it. After several attempts he was nowhere near success. When frustration started to show, I gave him a sheet of butter paper on which to trace the outlines. I told him to go over the outline several times first with a finger and then with a pencil to get an idea of its shape. In the end he was able to do it on his own. Unfortunately, each time after that when he came to a difficult drawing, he asked for the tracing paper! I had to make sure I lost it permanently to bring back his confidence. Ravi liked to use my clutch pencil for drawing. What he liked most about it was the sharpener. I had not known of its existence until then. I let him keep it.

All work was done in Hindi. One day Ravi's younger brother accompanied him and, in a bid to outdo Ravi, proceeded to write down things in English. Ravi could not bear to be upstaged like that. This was, after all his realm and his brother was just a visitor. He promptly copied down the whole thing in amazingly well crafted letters. He was after all an artist! The mother had probably thought that this way she would have time to rest but I did not look kindly upon this. It was bad for the mental and emotional well being of Ravi. Mrs. Reddy made sure Jai did not accompany Ravi after that and all was well with Ravi's world.

After some months, on an impulse, I decided to initiate Ravi into the world of sounds. The early words he uttered were crude and incomprehensible. Soon, however, there was a marked improvement. Only problem was that each time he was able to say some word reasonably clearly he would start to enlist all the words he could say and promptly voice them!

One evening, Ravi came along with his mother and after an elaborate bow handed me a lovely bouquet of roses. It was my birthday gift. Sometime earlier I had gifted Ravi some books on his birthday and he had asked me when mine was. He had remembered. I was deeply touched

For some time now I had been worried about Ravi's health. He seemed undernourished and was not as energetic as before. Immediately he arrived, he would sit down on the settee his hands clasping his temples. When I asked him what the matter was he would indicate his head was throbbing and his heart was thumping. I told his mother and grandmother that Ravi was undernourished. They said he was just putting on a show. Some days later, while at home, he crumbled to the ground and when he was taken to the doctor I was proved right. I was scared after that. At the same time I was happy he had fainted in his home not at my place. At the outset, he had liked having homemade snacks with the dip dip tea at my house but after a few days indicated he had been asked not to eat at my place. With such people one has to be careful.

School exams were round the corner. Ravi had to attend compulsory classes at the tutor's place. He would not be able to come until after the exams.

At the start of the vacations, Mrs. Reddy came and informed me that her husband had received a promotion and they were moving to Bombay. It was time to say "Goodbye" to the Sunshine Express.

For quite a while I missed Ravi. I had allowed myself to get too attached to the child. The glow on his face, his eagerness to come to me for studies and the pleasure both derived when we created our masterpieces, has brought home to me the fact that to cherish a child is more important than to have one. One must not stop loving children for fear of parting from them.

4

Whirlpool

The party had been enjoyable. Now for a good night's rest. That was not to be. Even as Jaya was about to insert the key in the lock, the door opened.

Surprised, she asked, "What, you are all still awake?" The three smiling people she had left at home were a picture of gloom. "Is anything wrong?" she asked.

"Everything. Sit down first," said Vijaya as she pulled her sister down onto the sofa beside her. Then she burst into uncontrollable weeping. Something was wrong.

Vikas was trying valiantly to hold back his tears; after all he was the man of the house. His little sister, Vani, was making every effort to turn invisible. She stood silent, head downcast. Something definitely was not right.

Horrible thoughts gnawed at Jaya's entrails. Vijaya's husband, Vivek, had just that evening left for Chandigarh. Had something happened to him?

"Is Vivek all right? Has he reached home? Did he ring?"

"Yes, yes he is all right," retorted Vikas with unusual stress on 'he'. He started pacing the floor cracking an imaginary whip.

"What a wonderful man! Goes to Shirdi and this is what he does!" Vikas was screaming. This was the first pointer. Vivek was the villain of the piece.

Jaya glanced at the wall clock. It was about to strike one. What will the neighbours say? But her sobbing sister put things in correct perspective.

Family first. She held Vijaya close until the sobbing subsided. She made Vikas sit on the other side and sat Vani on her lap. The little one was trembling like a leaf. Such emotional high drama is not good for the health of a seven year old. Secure in the arms of her aunt, Vani buried her nose into the ample bosom and fell into a fitful sleep. All this had been too much to handle.

Now there were just the two to tell the tale. Between the babble of the broken-hearted woman and the son whose idol had been cruelly shattered just when he needed it most, Jaya was, somehow, able to piece together what had happened. The tiniest of tiny nudges and the foundations on which the Gupta family had lived their dreams, so far, had collapsed. The hero had feet of clay.

Just two days before they were a story book family, vibrant, warm and deeply caring. Now all was over.

The pilgrimage to Shirdi was an annual ritual. It was a sort of thanksgiving, a part of family tradition. The mother and children were fun-loving people and the father had no choice but to join in. Left to himself, Vivek's favourite pastime was singing hymns in praise of the Creator. After the pilgrimage they had gone to Mumbai. It was to enjoy a brief spell before going back to the usual rut but the heavy rains had turned Mumbai into a watery hell. Train service suddenly stopped and they were stranded. This did not affect the mood of the Gupta family. They took it as an adventure. They were together, weren't they? Adolescence is the greatest adventure of all and young Vikas was on the threshold of this experience. It is the duty of a young son to take some burden off his father's shoulders. Vikas took the two heaviest bags, his mother took the suitcase and Vivek picked Vani up. They stepped off the train and headed for the bus stand warily. It almost ended in disaster as the swirling force of the floodwaters almost carried Vikas away. Vivek came to the rescue of his son and a calamity was narrowly averted. Vivek does not know swimming.

In Delhi the tale was told with gusto, all four supplying bits of information reliving the thrill. It was their biggest adventure and had to be narrated over and over. Vikas earned himself a lot of praise from his father and hugs from his mother and sister. As for Vivek, he was Superman, standing tall and pulling back his child from the clutches of certain death!

Now this!

As Vivek sat in the taxi listening to the last minute instructions of his loving wife, he suddenly remembered his briefcase. Vani was sent to fetch it. The case was not shut properly and something caught her eye. Full of curiosity, Vani took it out. It was the prettiest birthday card she had seen. It was addressed to Sunita and at the bottom in her Papa's hand were the words 'Love from guess who?'. Vivek, briefcase and card departed without event.

The card bothered Vani. Her father had never bought a card in his life and Vijaya had often chided him for that. Who was Sunita? Could it be Sunita aunty who taught Geography at her father's college? She grudgingly admitted that Sunita was pretty, but to send her a card? This mystery was no fun she decided. Better tell Mom before things got out of hand. She had a woman's instinct, young as she was! She told her mother. In the endnote of the card then lay the germs of betrayal.

Vijaya and Vivek both had colourful pasts and had been drawn to each other on the rebound having failed in their respective love affairs. They were sensitive friends willing to listen without being judgmental. She was the warmth he needed coming in from the cold. He was the strength that was vital for her to put things behind her and move on. They got married.

The teasing, the friendly banter carried on after marriage. To let her marriage go stale was not on Vijaya's agenda. Vijaya with her sultry charm was still attractive after all these years but she had found her Mr. Right. Vivek too seemed to be happily settled.

Vivek was easy-going and not too particular about his clothes and appearance. One day a visitor came to their house. After he had left, Vikas turned to his mother and wistfully asked, "Why can't Papa dress smartly like uncle?"

Vijaya was in a mood for fun and blithely countered, Shall we get a new father for you, smart and handsome like uncle Batra?"

The joke did not go well with Vikas. He was deeply devoted to his Papa, smartly dressed or not. He began to cry. He stopped only when Vijaya assured him," Why should we get a new Papa when yours is the best in the world!"

That brought the smile back, he realized his Mom was just joking. All was right with his world.

In a set-up where things were so transparent, secretiveness had no place. Vani didn't like it that her father had not told them about the card. Vikas didn't like the way the card had been signed off. Jaya didn't like it that, privy as they were to each other's secrets, Vivek had not told her about Sunita.

Seven agonizing hours had to be borne somehow before Vivek would get home and contact could be made. There were no mobile phones then. When at last they decided he would have got home, they found the STD locked. Jaya hadn't foreseen any emergency and had not bothered to unlock it before going to the wedding reception with her husband. Vikas went to the neighbourhood STD booth and rang his father. He said tersely," Ring Mom up, she is worried," and hung up.

When Vikas got home his mother was on the phone. She had obviously demanded an explanation and was not satisfied with the response. At both ends were persons unwilling to listen quietly and try to understand the other's stand. There was a lot Vijaya had to say but Vivek had put down the phone. She burst into helpless tears. The booth had shutdown at midnight. The family could do nothing but wait for the hosts to return from the party.

STD unlocked, a flurry of calls was made but Vivek did not answer. Had he gone to bed or was he just trying to avoid further inquisition.

Just then, a memory came, uncalled, from the shadows. In a fit of anger, at a trivial misdemeanor, Vivek had taken an over-dose of sleeping pills. Vikas had to rush to the neighbours' to get help. He was then just five and had forgotten the whole thing. Vijaya hadn't.

She took her sister aside and told her about it. Jaya was flabbergasted. Things were becoming too hot to handle and Jaya sought her husband's help.

So far, not wishing to invade Vijaya's privacy, Mohan had retired to his room. Now he rang up a close friend, Gaurav, who lived in Chandigarh and knew Vivek well too, and asked him to ring up Vivek as he was not responding and his wife was worried. Gaurav soon called back to say that Vivek had not answered his call either.

Mohan was truly unnerved now. It was close to three in the morning. Where was Vivek? More importantly, how was Vivek? He had no option but to request Gaurav to go over to Vivek's house in the morning to make sure all was well. Gaurav had not the foggiest notion what all the fuss was about, and to give him credit, never asked. He probably sensed something was wrong that was too personal to be disclosed to an outsider.

It would be a long night.

Vikas, meanwhile, had worked himself up further. First the treachery and now this attitude! He got back to cracking his imaginary whip in the fashion of an animal trainer at a circus. His father was now a villain beyond redemption. He had to be handed out his just rewards.

"Wait till I get home, you rogue, you saint, you mahatma. You are a good for nothing humbug. I've seen through you. I'll turn you out of the house. You have no right to live with us. Go to your Sunita, you rascal, ' he raved in between sobs.

He made verbal feints in the fashion of Don Quixote, "What? You will turn us out of the house? OK we will move to my grandfather's house. You can't turn us out from there, can you? That will be your punishment. You will clean the house and cook your own food then you will truly appreciate what my Mom does for you. Sunita! Bah!"

Unaware of the unspoken fears weighing on his mother's heart, he turned to Vijaya and said with finality, "Mom, we will not live with him. Divorce him!"

Jaya wanted to shake the child out of his shock but held her peace. Any child would have reacted this way. Besides, how would he know that the uppermost emotion in his mother's mind was now not anger but anguish, and fear.

Vijaya listlessly just responded, "Yes, yes. Calm down." She was worried for him. God knows what impact it might have on his tender mind. She was worried for Vani too. The child hadn't said much since she divulged the unpleasant secret. Vijaya knew she had been feigning sleep. Could she sleep while her brother was ranting and raving? Vani was a very sensitive little girl. She hated to hurt anyone and if she did so unwittingly she mooned over the incident for days on end. It was her family that she had hurt this time. She was weighed down with an unnamed guilt.

Jaya too was worried for both the children. One was screaming profanities and the other was quietly subdued. In addition there was Vijaya, poor thing, how would she handle the situation. She was angry with Vivek for bringing this on her sister. More than that, she was worried about him. "Hope he has done nothing stupid to himself, " she prayed silently.

Vikas turned to his aunt for support, "Mom must divorce the man, mustn't she? He is a cheat. We can't live with him," he declared with finality.

Jaya knew this was the last thing Vijaya was thinking about. Hurt had taken a back seat. If her husband was well, all else would sort itself out in due course. Jaya gently reminded Vikas that his parents had married because they loved each other a lot and such talk would hurt his Mom.

Vikas retorted, "That's true but he now loves Sunita. He doesn't need us anymore, neither do we need him!"

The fear that Vivek, unable to cope with the situation, might have done something desperate just would not go away. She lit a lamp before Lord Ganesh.

There was nothing to do but wait for the morning. Jaya crossed her fingers and made a silent prayer. She would feed eleven poor children if Vivek was OK.

The darkness of the night had seeped into their hearts and minds. Jaya shifted in with her sister and the kids. No one slept. Jaya kept going from bed to bed comforting the three by turns. Vikas muttered and mumbled all the time. Vijaya sobbed and blew her nose almost incessantly.

At one point Vani whispered in her aunt's ear, "Do you think I should have kept quiet about the card?"

"No, my little one, you did just right. These things are for adults to handle not children," assured Jaya.

Vani seemed relieved, yet there was a niggling doubt still in her mind, "But I've made everyone so sad!"

"Things will become all right once you get to Chandigarh."

"Will they, really?"

"Of course they will. Just like old times."

There was one last doubt to be cleared. "Papa will hate me. He will think I am a tattle- tale. Am I one? My teacher at school says that is very bad, almost as bad as lying."

Jaya wondered if telling about the card had been so bad what would not telling have done to the tender mind in the long run. She was glad for the child that she had chosen to speak out.

Morning brought an early call. Gaurav had made his promised visit. Vivek was surprised to see Gaurav so early in the morning but the latter said he was out for a walk and just decided to check things out as the light was on in the inner rooms and he was under the impression that Vivek and his family were out of station. That seemed to satisfy Vivek. They had breakfast together.

Jaya was relieved the storm had blown over. The children were sound asleep after the troubled night. Vijaya seemed more at peace with herself though her morning was still some way off. This night will come to haunt her again and again. Will the tender minds of the children be permanently blighted or will the resilience of childhood come to their rescue and the whole episode fade away gradually? Will Vivek regain his position as hero in their hearts?

5

Narayani

"Narayani!" the very walls of her home sang out joyously, "Narayani!" Tinkling bells of *payals* and jingling of glass bangles called back, "Here I am, here I am!" A symphony of peals of laughter announced, "Here I am, here I am!"

The only sister of two brothers, she was sent by God to be showered with love. The lives of her parents, her *chacha* and *chachi*, her brothers and their wives revolved round her. Fun loving, cheerful and chirpy— that was Narayani. Love was a two-way process in this joint family. A fevered brow and Narayani was there with ice-cold water and soft towels. A headache had to take its leave fast; Narayani's famous tulsi leaf tea and all-purpose balm had that magic. Both the *bhabhis* loved her. She did things with their make-up that got them appreciative 'Wows'. The *mehndi* patterns and cleverly arranged *bindis*, the flower *gajras* were uniquely hers and made her *bhabhis* the centre of attraction at parties. Nor was this all, she helped with chores around the house and some of these were specially kept aside for her like the arrangement of flowers in vases and decoration of the salad platter. Her mother and *chachi* always found the vegetables chopped and ready for cooking. It was Narayani who always answered the doorbell and the home-comer was greeted with a glass of cold water. She had a very neat hand and artistic eye and could pick a new knitting pattern in a jiffy so the winter season began with each member of the family flaunting a brand new sweater or cardigan made by Narayani.

The *bhabhis* on their part were constantly on the lookout for bits of jewellery or some smart dress for their darling. It wasn't as if they were trying to out do each other. That was not the style of this home. Everything was planned and done together. The surprise element suffered a bit, but hey, who cares everyone enjoyed it!

Each festival was celebrated with gusto but *Rakhi* was special. The brothers would pretend they had forgotten to bring her gifts and she would pretend to pout and they would tease her a bit and then their wives would hand her the wonderful things they had chosen with love and care. For the brothers she was the best sister in the world and Narayani prayed fervently that in each birth she got them as brothers.

Narayani's father, Shyamlal, was not too well placed but it was he who had seen to the education of not only his sons but also his younger brother, Shivlal who went on to become an advocate. The elder son, Vijay, was an engineer and the younger, Vinay, a doctor. This is an old story and women, even the fairly well educated, did not take up jobs. So was it with this family too. Women looked to the smooth running of the home, saw to it that each member was well looked after, shared in the decision making of important issues and ensured that the next generation got their family values. Shyamlal headed the family together with his wife. They were loved and respected and it was understood whatever they decided upon ultimately would be for the common good. Such was the faith they had in him.

Good times fly by and soon the little girl was a young woman and the entire family had but one concern — how to get a prince charming for their beloved Narayani. Now we come to a little detail not hitherto disclosed. Narayani was not very pretty. This, one might say, was of little import as she had so many good qualities in her. Any young man would have been lucky to marry her. Unfortunately, even those days, a girl had to be a paragon of beauty whatever her intrinsic merit. A distant relative had heard of a young man who she thought would make a good match for Narayani. He was just into law practice. Maybe Shivlal could have him as his junior. The young man, the relative revealed, had actually shown a lot of interest in the match.

So it was that Hari Prasad came with his mother, Vasudha, and sister, Kanta, to see Narayani. A girl rarely got to see the boy those days as her eyes did not dare to look up! Narayani brought in the sherbet and eats and sat down beside her elder *bhabhi*, Savita. This was the third time someone had come to see her and she was trembling. What if this man too rejected her? She wanted to run out of the room and have a good sob. Savita put her arm across her shoulders and held her close to put her at her ease.

Pretty soon the go between informed Shyamlal that Narayani had met with their approval and they could go ahead with the wedding preparations. Not much had to be done as Shyamlal believed in simple wedding ceremonies. Shivlal, Vijay and Vinay all had austere weddings. Why waste the girl's father's money was his constant chant. Is happiness dependent on false pomp and show? Hari Prasad went along with the idea. It was thought this was because he had recently lost his father and did not want too much festivity.

A glum-faced Kanta received Narayani at her sasural. Things did not auger well

Narayani beseeched all the gods to help her. Her whole family would be heart broken should she have an unhappy marriage. Her relations with her *bhabhis* had always been so full of love that she could not imagine that her own *nanad* should look upon her with any other sentiment. Not a smile touched the lips of either mother-in-law or sister-in-law throughout the ceremonies. What was the matter?

Family status, and not so much the beauty of the girl, counted those days and if most wedding guests thought Narayani plain they did not comment. Hari Prasad's mother was a cunning woman, surely she must have compensated for that with a heavy dowry they speculated. Inwardly all sympathised with the bride. She seems a sweet natured young girl. They hoped Vasudha and Kanta would treat her well.

For any girl the first day at her in-laws is one of unease and uncertainty. Would they like her? More importantly, would her husband like her? Dreams fight for place with fears unknown. For Narayani the hours crawled by. Maybe the night would be different. Narayani had been a little girl when Vijay got married so her recollections were a bit faint but by the time her second *bhabhi*, Prema, came, she was well into her teens and had helped decorate the bridal room with sweet-smelling flowers. She had been so excited that her feet hardly touched the ground. Here, she discerned a decided chill. Once again her heart began to sink.

By eleven o' clock the last of the sleepy guests had left and it was the time for her to be taken to the bridal room. A shy look around the cluttered room did nothing to raise her sagging spirits. A bride may not complain so she sat down gingerly on the crumpled sheet that covered the rickety bed. She waited and waited. The room was dark but the grand clock in the adjoining hall where the guests were sleeping told her it was one o'clock.

There was still no sign of Hari Prasad. She must have dozed off after that tired as she was after the long journey from Agra to Hathras and sitting through the ceremony at which visitors came to see her and give her gifts. The blast of alcohol brought her home to reality. Her groom had come and he was drunk. Narayani stood up in a fluster not knowing what to do or say. It was nothing like shown in pictures. All the tales about '*suhag raat*' she heard from friends had not prepared her for this. He will make love to you—no details were provided and Narayani would not know, at least not tonight. Her husband lay sprawled on the bed fast asleep. Quietly she took off his shoes and socks, spread the coverlet on the ground, and lay down. She dreamt she was being chased by demons through a deep forest. The crowing of a cock awoke her. Her husband had left the room.

Kanta came into the room a little while later. She had a queer leer on her lips. There was not much of love, as Narayani knew it, in her behaviour towards her newly wed and only *bhabhi*. Nostalgia started to gnaw at her heart. Her thoughts went back to her own *bhabhis*. They must be having tea and talking about her. How could she tell? The hiccups that had started had stopped as soon as she thought of them. That said it all, didn't it?

This curious behaviour went on for three days. There was just one small change. A lamp with a zero watt bulb had been put in her room and she could now spend the hours counting lizards as they feasted on the tiny insects that infested the place.

There were whispered insinuations amongst the guests and Narayani did not know what to make of them. She felt ashamed of herself, her new family and her total helplessness in dealing with it. By the third day all guests had left. From the look of things, it seemed things were heading towards a showdown. She hoped her brother who was coming to take her home would not know of it. He was hot blooded and would not have his sister maltreated.

She had to get her box packed before his arrival. She had been told by her mother not to do anything without her mother-in-law's approval. The three family members were in the courtyard. Narayani touched Vasudha's feet and asked, "Ma, what things should I pack to take home?"

Before Vasudha could respond, Hari Prasad yelled, "Take away everything you brought. God knows it was not much. I was a fool to marry you. Your uncle is great! He has a beautiful wife and what do I get, an ugly witch!" He stomped out of the room. Narayani could not believe her ears but she held her peace.

Kanta was next. "Hari Bhaiya has been unfairly treated. We had thought such a plain girl would at least bring a big dowry. Your uncle is rich but it seems your father said he would not accept any help from him. What can a pauper give his daughter? And to think *bhaiya* had assured me that I would lack nothing as everything he got would be passed on to me at my marriage!"

"We are ruined!" lamented the mother-in-law. "Don't stand there sobbing. Your brother will be here shortly and we don't want any swollen eyes, do we? When you get home tell your *chacha*, not your father, you stupid girl, that you can come back to this house only if you bring twenty thousand rupees. Understand?"

Narayani was dumbfounded. She had never heard such talk back home. Her elder *bhabhi* was Shyamlal's best friend's daughter. On his deathbed the friend had handed over responsibility of Savita to him," Please get her married to a decent boy." It hadn't taken long for Shyamlal to decide that Savita should marry his own son, Vijay. Here she would get love and there would be no dowry hassles. A simple function was arranged and Savita became the beloved *bahu* of the Lal family. In the marriages of Shivlal and Vinay too no dowry was taken. Narayani had always seen her *bhabhis* happy.

This was just the beginning of Narayani's horror story. The fairytale was over

The two *bhabhis* saw her and instinctively knew something was terribly wrong. A bit of probing and the sordid game plan spilled out. Shivlal burst out, "The double-faced wretch, he will pay for this. I will take him to court." Shyamlal suggested that it would be enough to let Hari know that his activities were being watched. When Narayani returned to her husband's house she was given ten thousand by Vijay. The money was grabbed greedily.

The lady who had earlier brought the proposal was grieved that Hari had turned out to be a rogue. She thought the money should not have been given; it would only whet their greed. She hit out at Vasudha, "I am ashamed I even thought of Hari as a good match. Neither he nor your family deserves Narayani. Remember, God sees everything."

It was a very strange situation. The family of three slept in the long verandah while Narayani continued to sleep in the cubbyhole. No attempt had been made to consummate the marriage. When Narayani wanted to join the others in the verandah, Hari dithered, "What will Ma and Kanta think of us? Have you no shame?"

It was hot that night, Narayani got up for a glass of water. Strange noises were coming from the verandah so she went to look. The brother and sister were in bed together. No wonder the sister would feel bad seeing her brother and his bride sleep together. That was why Hari did not need his bride. His needs were already being fulfilled. Vasudha seemed to be in deep slumber. That was amazing. The most sacred of relationships had been desecrated. Narayani was nauseated. Now she wanted no relationship with this man. Her flesh crawled at the thought of his vile touch. The act she had unwittingly witnessed was so shameful that Narayani did not tell anyone of it. The truth is her lips could not bear to utter the abominable truth; it would enrage and sadden all who mattered to her

Torture was a way of life with Hari. He wanted the marriage to end without anyone suspecting anything. The next time he took her to her parents' home all were shocked to see her arm in plaster. She told her mother that scared of monkeys she fled downstairs and tripped. Her younger *bhabhi* smelt a rat and ultimately Narayani broke down and disclosed that Hari had pushed her off the head of the staircase.

Hari did not know his secret was out. Emboldened, he worked on another nefarious plan. He took Narayani out for a walk to the local park. On the way there was a small lake with a pretty bridge. As they crossed the bridge Hari shoved her off the side. People who had been watching rushed to the place. By then Narayani had swum across. Hari had been unaware that his wife could swim. The throng had just begun to beat up the villain and Narayani once again resorted to a lie. She told the assembled people that her foot had slipped and Hari was in fact trying to save her. Hari knew his schemes had to be subtle; Narayani's uncle was an advocate.

As it chanced, soon after, Narayani came down with typhoid and was promptly dispatched to her father's; looking after a sick person was too much work.

All those days she was sick, one *bhabhi* or other was with her and tale after tale of torture, neglect and incest crawled out from her bleeding heart. What had the villain done to their darling?

With tender care Narayani at last recovered. Left to herself she would have preferred to die but such matters are not for us to decide.

Hari came to see how Narayani was doing. He peeped into the room. His wife was pale but seemed better. The doctor was just leaving. Hari decided to have a word with him.

"Is that a man or a monster?" fumed the doctor

"What is the matter, Doctor Sahib, why are you so agitated? What has upset you?" enquired Shyamlal.

The doctor's face was red with anger. "Your son-in-law is Satan-incarnate. He came up to me and do you know what?"

"What?"

"He complained that I had deprived him of the chance of a second marriage!"

It was then decided that Narayani was not to go back. Sadly, she had a relapse and died a month later.

God above has His own code of justice. It might be delayed but ultimately catches up. So was it with Hari.

He married his sister off and got himself a second wife. This one was pretty and out of a sense of insecurity Hari would not let her go to her parental home. There was another reason. If they wanted their daughter so much they probably would be more attuned to his demands for money. The second wife too died within two years and Hari was determined to do better the third time round. A proposal did come but things were not moving fast enough so Hari decided to go incognito and find out things for himself.

He passed himself off as Hari Prasad's friend. After a while the talk moved in the direction of the proposed alignment. He enquired," So, what's the delay?"

"Oh! We have heard the man is eccentric!"

"Eccentric?"

"We have even heard he is a nutcase. He treated both his wives badly."

"They say he is just a step away from the mad house," broke in a third. "We would be stupid to marry our daughter off to him!"

That did the trick! "So this is the canard being spread about me! I am eccentric, am I? I am a nutcase, am I? I am just a step away from the madhouse, am I?" raving thus Hari prasad left the bewildered host. When they understood what had happened, they burst out laughing.

When the hand of God strikes it really hurts. Some years later Narayani's people got word that Hari Prasad was dead. He had become raving mad and was found dead in a gutter, filthy and naked.

Narayani had been avenged.

6

Laukhi

Laukhi came from Bisan Charlie in Assam. Just as Laukhi is the degenerated form of Laxmi so also Bisan Charlie is the colloquial form of Vishwanath Chariyalaya meaning Lord Siva is omnipresent. She had been brought to Delhi to work as house-help at Mrs. Panda's place. Before that she worked as casual labourer on a tea plantation, that is when she was not engaged in augmenting the family resources brewing illicit country liquor! Two years back when she made her appearance in this big bad city, she had a fresh, dew-washed face that comes with close communion with Nature, and it showed. Pretty may not have been the word for the waif-like creature clad in a worn-out frock but there was the charm of shy innocence. Add to it a clumsy way of carrying herself and a complete ignorance of urbane behaviour.

The next two years were learning time for Laukhi. To begin with, she learnt to keep herself clean. Gradually, she progressed to simple and cheap ways of grooming. The previously undefined features slowly gave way to chiseled beauty and the gauche tribal girl matured into a somewhat sophisticated Delhite. She had learnt to speak a bit of Oriya and Hindi, could commute alone to the local market and handle a short list of purchases with aplomb. The initial hunger for good food had been satiated as she was now sure of her next meal, its quantity and quality. The large helping of rice had given way to small portions of this, that and the other. The frock had been replaced with a salwar suit.Here she didn't have to *go to the bush* and had, to herself, a western style toilet that she soon learnt to keep clean.

Laukhi soon made a few friends amongst the maids in the colony. If she had male friends back home, she had been properly warned against such misadventures in Delhi. The first whiff of a scandal and she would be packed off back to Assam!

While in Assam, Laukhi had not been a keen on school and who could blame her, an orphan under pressure to earn her daily fistful of rice. Here, she was taught the rudiments of Hindi and made conversant with simple arithmetic so as to be able to deal with the shopkeepers. Best of all she learnt to embroider daintily.

Laukhi was the bright star in her milieu. The other maids could not even recognise the letters of the alphabet and here she was able to read and write short sentences. She basked in the glory! That this was the result of Mrs. Panda's painstaking effort was, at times, coolly forgotten.

The months and years flitted by and now it was time to pay a visit to her village that is in the middle of nowhere. Veena, her friend and escort, was better placed in this regard. Her village snuggled up to the highway. Her home was a comfortable kilometer off the road so she was carrying a lot of goodies in a huge tin trunk. Laukhi was not about to be left behind; she had her brother's family that she loved a lot. Each delicacy served to her, brought her nephews and niece to mind. The life of penury and deprivation they led was in stark contrast with the life of plenty she now lived. At times it seemed sinfully extravagant. She just had to carry some *ghee* and good refined oil! She bought a fairly large tin trunk and a backpack. Each time she went to the local market she came back with an assortment of clothes and trinkets. She was not wasteful like one born to wealth. Carefully she tried to maximise the funds available. In addition, by now, she had a large store of hand-me-downs that she no longer needed as she got two new dresses each year and with her handsome pay could afford to buy almost anything she set her heart upon. These old clothes, she told herself matter-of-factly, were fifty times better (that was as far as she could count) than what they currently wore. Each day she reminded herself that she would have to carry the heavy trunk on her head but next market day it was the same story. The backpack threatened to give way at the seams and had to be supplemented with a large sling bag. Still she felt she might not have done enough!

There was one big problem. Veena's people wanted her to get married and it was feared it might be the same in Laukhi's case. Having tasted the good life of the metro, neither girl wanted to stay back home permanently. A full stomach and clean clothes would by themselves have been motivation enough. In addition, now, they had the power that a full purse gives. They could shower, hitherto unthinkable, gifts on their loved ones. The treats, for all we know, could be their subtle way of ensuring another lease of city life. After all the families would benefit, wouldn't they?

Laukhi was warmly received. The clothes she had bought for the children, she found to her horror, were two sizes too small but she was equal to the situation. She would keep them for the new additions to the extended family. For her nephews and niece she would give money. It was a welcome option.

Festival cheer lasts only as long as the food on the table. Laukhi had taken a lot of gifts but they wanted more. All her money was taken to buy an adjoining piece of land. The clothes she bought for her own use were also taken away. After all she was going back to the land of plenty where she would soon build up a fresh stock! Laukhi bore it all patiently. She just bided her time patiently.

Back in Delhi, as the month drew to a close, Mrs. Panda's anxiety began to show. A temporary help is no substitute for a fulltime maid. Distance makes the heart grow fonder; Mrs. Panda's case was no exception. Each little virtue Laukhi had, multiplied manifold, came with a rush of nostalgia. There was no denying the girl was sweet, loving and hard working. Besides, Mrs. Panda had become so dependant on Laukhi that making a simple cup of tea was a chore and it didn't turn out quite as tasty!

Veena sent word that she would probably not come back. That was bad news. It meant someone else would have to escort Laukhi back. She still could not travel by herself. A quick message was sent through Veena. The to and fro fare of Laukhi's escort would be paid but she must come immediately. That had the desired effect. Laukhi and her brother, Ram, were at the door after a fortnight. For the brother it was a free ride to this beautiful city and Mrs. Panda was so relieved that she packed him a generous hamper for his return journey.

Unlike her early days, this time round Laukhi did not pine for the family. She was determined to settle down and make Delhi her home. Besides, she had so many things to learn. She must begin with learning to write letters. That would truly impress the other maids and her people back home. Now she spent a lot of time reading out of the primary course books bought for her. She felt important and loved to show off her newfound reading and writing skills to any one who showed any interest. She had a very neat handwriting. She learnt to knit too for after all she would need a sweater in the cold of Delhi and why buy one when she could make one.

Her embroidered handkerchiefs were snapped up as soon as she finished them giving her both money and satisfaction.

This went on for some time but her desire for learning was skin deep. It was not for its own sake, merely to impress her peer group. Besides, her over-enthusiasm did not go well with her employer. As soon as Mrs. Panda's head touched the pillow for a well-deserved siesta, Laukhi would be by her bedside with some problem or other she had with her sums. Eagerness to teach turned to irritation. Laukhi's fervour too cooled off soon after and she became a maid like any other.

There was a fresh development in Laukhi's village. Her sister died leaving behind two children. Naturally everybody thought of Laukhi. Who could be a better mother to them than their own aunt? For Laukhi this was an unnerving proposal. It entailed several issues, all of them unpalatable. She would have to marry a person ten years older than her. They would be totally incompatible. He would not come to the city leaving his farms and she could not go back to the rural life. It was one thing visiting her village and another living there forever. She was now a city girl with city ways. Going to the bush, dining on leaves and roots, brewing country liquor, cooking on a log fire without a pressure cooker would be too painful. Besides, Laukhi had tasted women's lib. She had seen her sister and sister-in-law being beaten by their husbands. She was determined this was not going to be her life.

She was to leave for her village in a week. She had to do something, and fast.

For sometime a young man had been sending her proposals of marriage through a maid in the same colony. Each time she went to the market, and the trips had increased somewhat, he was there with some tiny trinket or a gift of some sweet she loved. He was a sales boy at one of the shops. Laukhi was in a bind. She remembered her employer's warning. Also she needed sound advice. She decided to confide in her mistress.

Mrs. Panda called the man and the inquisition revealed he was married. His wife had died leaving behind three tiny kids. They were being taken care of by their grandmother but it was a temporary arrangement. Once Deepak, that was the man's name, married Laukhi, the children would be the responsibility of their stepmother. Mrs. Panda advised Laukhi to go home as planned and study the situation at her sister's place. As the two proposals seemed similar she should look into them in depth and marry only after that.

There was one hazy area. Deepak lived in a jhuggi and there would not be any toilet. Laukhi would have to go to an adjoining teak plantation. These last facts were kept secret or so Laukhi vouched later. However this is doubtful for a day before her scheduled departure for Vishwanath Charyalaya, Laukhi went to the market on the pretext of some last minute purchases. She did not return. Next morning she rang up to inform Mrs. Panda that she had married Deepak and would be coming after a few days for her blessings. Mrs. Panda put the phone down in a huff.

Laukhi was playing the innocent to the hilt! She did know about the toilet facilities and quality of living space. The plan to stay away for a few days was to ensure that her brother, tired of waiting, would have left by then. Among the Munda tribals, a woman was free to choose her husband. Laukhi had decided whom she wanted to marry and that was that! Ram would soon see there was no point in waiting for Laukhi to return.

For Mrs. Panda it was not a happy situation. Ram, instead of being thankful had not liked Mrs. Panda's interference. As a matter of fact he held her responsible for his sister's waywardness. Anyway, who was she to advise Laukhi on matters of marriage? Now the silly girl had eloped with this good for nothing fellow who had nothing to offer her. Her brother-in-law had good paddy fields. If it was marriage she wanted why couldn't she have married her brother-in-law and looked after her sister's children instead of playing stepmother to Deepak's children? He had a point there. Ram went away very angry.

Mrs. Panda was too angry with Laukhi to give her blessings or, for that matter, anything. If Laukhi had done as told she would have been given a lot of gifts to help her settle down, now she would get nothing.

It took some time for Mrs. Panda to forgive the misdeed. She decided she could manage without fulltime help. The previous arrangement too had its minus points. As for Laukhi, she could visit once in a while but would not be given back her work.

Laukhi's stepchildren came twice but the grandmother would not trust them to Laukhi's care permanently so they went back. After a few abortions, no doubt at the behest of Deepak, Laukhi has at last given birth to a baby boy and is fairly content.

Last month she even went to her village with husband and baby to get the blessings of her brother. Her brother-in-law has married again and has a new baby girl from his new wife. Life goes on. Amazingly, Laukhi has never once blamed God for her travails. She has borne all courageously, after all she has been responsible for her own destiny and knows one must lie on the bed one makes, roses or thorns. The Munda girl has not come a long way maybe but is determined her son shall have a proper education and do his mother proud.

7

Baba's birthday gift

For the nth time Vivek went through his wardrobe, a medley of cheap new clothes and expensive old ones. What should he wear for the small party he was throwing for his closest friends to celebrate his twenty-first birthday?

Rajkumar would be there, no doubt resplendent in a new suit. How the name suited him, the great show off! But, he had a heart of gold and had stood by him during the ups and downs destiny had heaped on him. In a way, Rajkumar was his closest pal and it was to him Vivek turned when in need of a shoulder to cry on.

Rajkumar's father had a high-end furniture showroom and it was understood that he would join the family business when he finished studies. Rajkumar had a full wallet and a generous heart and Vivek was the principal beneficiary. Vivek , on his part was a man of pride and hated even the thought that he may be sponging on his friend or taking advantage of his fondness for him but he was also fond of the good things of life and eating out was an expensive pastime that could not be sustained on a lean allowance. So, Rajkumar took it on himself to pick up the restaurant bills.

However, this did not solve the immediate problem

Then, there would be Raman, brilliant but self-effacing. Simply dressed himself, he hardly noticed what the others were wearing. Vivek and he became friends in class eight. Raman's family was full of professors and school teachers and laid more store by matters of the intellect than material values. He did not go into raptures over the fancy stuff Vivek's father, Dr. Hari Prasad Singh, bought From department stores on Oxford Street,

London, en route from Kano, on his rare visits home from Nigeria and now when Vivek's family had suffered setbacks due to poor business deals, he did not notice the change! To him a friend is a friend, not a pair of frayed jeans.

Above all, it was Deepak's views that mattered. He was the foil against which his own virtues glowed resplendent! To Deepak, Vivek was the hero. He copied his style of talking and devil-may-care swagger. Deepak's father was a chemist with a small dispensary and could ill-afford to provide his son with the luxuries his friends seemed to have. Vivek needed him for the unstinted adoration and loyalty. Deepak seemed not to have noted the gradual degradation in Vivek's wardrobe or, maybe, it was more suited to his own financial status and he was secretly glad of the change that lifted a load off his mind and purse. He was also the one to compliment Vivek when he was smartly dressed.

Ultimately, Vivek decided on a, still serviceable, St. Michael's shirt and sports jacket. The silk tie from the Central Cottage Industries Emporium, Delhi, bought on a school trip, would go well with it. Stepping into adulthood, he wanted to appear trim and proper. Looks were important to Vivek and he assumed they were so to others also. He hoped he would at least look all ready to face life even if he didn't quite feel so! Quirks of fate had dealt him so many blows that he didn't feel very optimistic despite his basically extrovert nature. He had hoped his father would be there for the celebrations but the latter had, instead, sent a greetings telegram! That was life. Not a soul in the world who cared.

The early years had been the only ones of unmixed prosperity and bliss. His grandfather, Thakur Chandra Bhan Singh, whom Vivek lovingly called 'Baba', had forty acres of agricultural land, two citrus orchards, a haveli in the village and two large kothies in Agra. Thakur Sahib was a simple, hardworking and affectionate man. He was tall, dark, handsome and imposing. He was sincere in his relationships and many were the people who swore by his generosity. The two city houses were permanently occupied by an assortment of relatives for whom cartloads of foodgrain and fruit were despatched at regular intervals as were tins of homemade ghee.

Vivek being the only grandchild was particularly doted upon. He was the apple of Baba's eyes. Baba had no inhibitions as he crawled on the floor on all fours with the toddler astride as they played 'donkey, donkey'. As he grew up, Baba took him on sightseeing trips which the two enjoyed immensely. Vivek's father was far away in distant Nigeria and phone calls were tedious and expensive. The purdah system prevalent in the region further cemented the bond. Even when his mother wanted something, Vivek was the go-between!

Vivek was a weakling as a babe and Baba was convinced his sole salvation lay in outdoor activities and the consumption of laddoos made with ghee. So, Vivek accompanied the cowherd in the morning when he took the cattle out for grazing in the nearby woods. Though today his ears turn pink when he is reminded of it, he had definitely enjoyed his rides on the back of Bholi the docile buffalo as she lumbered lazily in her quiet quest for juicy grass. He learnt to climb trees and loved to swing from the supple branches of the mango tree in the village chaupal determined to be as tall as his Baba. Time flew by happily.

When Vivek turned eight, Baba decided the village school was not enough for his growing needs and decided to shift to one of the city abodes so as to be able to supervise his grandson's education. He was in a quandary as to who would look after the farms and before taking the momentous decision wrote to his son to come home and take charge. "What is the point in teaching agriculture techniques to others when your own fields don't get the benefit of your learning?" The other alternative offered was that he should come back and take up a job in the city and do his duty by his wife and growing son and Thakur Sahib would look after the fields. The letter went unanswered regarding the main issue but was filled with a lot of talk of the appreciation he was getting for his work there and the impending promotion which he hoped to get the next year. No way was Dr. Hari Prasad Singh going to be coaxed out of his comfort zone. He was enjoying his sojourn in Nigeria and would continue there as long as possible! Thakur Chandra Bhan Singh understood that he would have to cope with things as best he could.

The village property was put under the care of a needy cousin. Getting the kothi vacated was difficult and ultimately the sycophants had to be paid a tidy sum. Finally, hakur Sahib, his daughter-in-law, grandson and the trusty cook addressed as 'Maharaj' took up abode in the kothi at Dilli Darwaza. Getting admission was no problem as the school was the Alma Mater of Dr. Singh who had done his school proud by standing second in the region in the high school board exams. Generosity, they say gets paid back in generosity but not so in Thakur Sahib's case. The occupants of the other kothi decided to usurp it and a very reluctant Thakur sahib had to drag them to court. It was only after three and a half years that he was restored his property. What had been a grand old mansion was now but a dilapidated apology for one. Baba's trust in humanity had been truly shattered and he spun a cocoon round himself. Vivek was his only hope and sole source of joy.

On the village scene, all went well in the beginning. The grain produce was sent on time as were canisters of ghee and baskets of fruit. Gradually, however, the needy cousin became a greedy one and a major part of the yield was sold off privately in the village itself and only a trickle made its way to Agra. Once again Thakur Sahib sent an SOS to his son. In reply he wrote he would be staying on for at least six more years and anyway he was not cut out for a career in a tiny hole of a village or a dingy little place called Agra!

Vivek felt Baba's hurt even though Baba tried to maintain a cool facade. Baba hid all financial difficulties from his family. His son had started remitting some money to ease his guilty conscience but Baba refused to take even a paisa from it. Dr Singh never bothered himself with such petty details as to where the funds to maintain his family were coming from. All the remitted money was put into fixed deposit schemes. Indeed, if he had come to know how the old man had been defrauded of his property, he would have berated him for his lack of business acumen. After all would it not cut into the size of his inheritance!

Vivek was doing well in school. This was a great consolation. The day his board result was out, Baba's joy knew no bounds. He distributed ten kilo pedas to neighbours and sent boxes of pure ghee sweets to all of Vivek's teachers. Vivek was given a moped as reward. Each time Thakur Sahib was visited by a friend he sent for Vivek and as the latter bowed to touch their feet they blessed and praised him and commented on his fine upbringing. Vivek did not know if he was more proud of his good marks or of this grand old man! He was determined to do his best by his Baba. He would ensure that in his old age he should not want anything.

However, this was not to be

The very next year a very dejected Dr. Singh came back home lock stock and barrel. Despite demonetisation, Nigerian economy was on a downward slide. Everything was exorbitantly expensive. With so little on their platter they could hardly be expected to open up their hearts to expatriates. His contract had not been renewed.

Life in Nigeria had been an unending round of social activities. Bored with the sedate life of Agra, Dr. Singh ferreted out old acquaintances in the hope that some semblance of high society life would be revived. Having lived so long without his family it never occurred to him that there was an immense difference in his and their lifestyles. His wife was in for a very tough time. She had never ventured out of purdah. Shopping for the daily needs was done by Baba, Vivek and Maharaj. Her personal needs were few. The occasional sari, bangles and sindoor she purchased on her visits to her parental home in Aligarh. Now here was her husband making, what seemed to her, all sorts of unreasonable demands on her. He had bought silly dresses in London, he called them gowns, and expected her to wear them when she accompanied him to, of all the places, clubs! She, who did not even step out of the door to hand over the garbage to the cleaner. "There are so many people to do it why should the bahu do it?" demanded Baba.

Unused to intellectual company, she would be tongue-tied and resented her husband's upbraiding in front of others. She who had been queen of her household was now a nitwit.

She was not the only one to suffer. The faithful Maharaj was like a family member. His cooking had been so far highly acclaimed by one and all. He was now unfairly scolded. He was a Brahmin and wore a dhoti while cooking food. This did not go well with the newfound sensibilities of Dr. Singh. "Why can't he wear a uniform and chef's cap?" he demanded. The daily fare of dal roti and vegetables he found inadequate but Maharaj had never cooked Chinese or Continental food. The family and some friends sniggered behind Dr. Singh's back but were too well-bred to say anything to his face.

Soon it became clear that Maharaj was redundant since he couldn't cook non-vegetarian dishes! This was a strictly vegetarian family. Meat was out of bounds. No one had ever eaten meat even at a restaurant. When the bickering became unbearable, Baba came up with a feasible solution. An outhouse was converted into an additional kitchen and a Khansama appointed. The family peace was secured as also the services of Maharaj who was threatening to quit. This meant additional burden on Thakur Sahib's purse but at least the family was together and happy.

Dr. Singh prided himself on his business acumen but if truth be told, he knew nothing about such matters. Now instead of helping out with family expenses, he decided to invest part of his considerable savings in shares. Valuable hours were spent in studying the trends of different shares but when shares did change hands, it was mostly to his disadvantage as he soon discovered! However, by now it was an intoxication he could not free himself of.

Around this time Thakur sahib once again urged his son to take over the running of the farms or else they would be lost forever. Seeing no response he resigned himself to his lot after all he was too old to look after things and if his son was not interested, the actual tillers might as well take the land for keeps.

Gradually, Dr. Singh's situation worsened perceptibly and he turned to Mr. Malhotra who had been in Nigeria with him. Many were the nights they had gone to clubs together. Mr. Malhotra suggested that they should open an armature rewinding workshop. The rose-tinted glasses prevented Dr. Singh from noticing that everything at stake would be his and any benefits accruing thereof would be shared equally. Machinery was bought and the spare kothi renovated. Part of it would be used as workshop and the rest as residence for the Manager, Mr. Malhotra!

Thakur Sahib tried to point out the pitfalls but was shut up. It was not his money he was told and how could a doddering old fool be expected to have the vision to envisage the prospects that lay ahead. By now even common courtesies had been cast aside. Thakur Sahib cut himself off from his son's affairs and tried to turn his attention to those of his grandson but Vivek had moved on and away. Now he had no time for Baba and, taking a leaf off his father's book, took all credit for his own success. Baba was out of touch with modern ways, he thought, and was needlessly overbearing and interfering. Nevertheless, Baba was still main financial support. He knew that he didn't need to butter up Baba as he did his father. A doleful expression did the trick. Those days a hundred rupee note went a long way and Vivek was sure of this bounty each time he went to take leave of Baba before going back to college. As Baba's resources diminished, so did the bounty and with it the frequency of visits.

Son and grandson now had little time now for the old, and now frail, man. The daughter-in-law, the one person who cared unconditionally, died of ulcers unable to cope with the stresses of the new lifestyle and the avalanche of setbacks. Nothing now bound them to the house which was no more a home.

Nobody realised that the constant cough that seemed to have pinned down the old man to his bed was anything more than a mild irritant. A worried Maharaj nursed him as best he could but soon felt the need to call the doctor. It was too late. Thakur Sahib had developed pneumonia. By the end of the third day he was no more.

The funeral rites afforded Dr. Singh and Vivek an opportunity to showcase closeness for the departed they no longer felt. The Maharaj left soon after. There was no place for him and the khansama took charge of their lives.

As days went by, the armature-rewinding venture turned into a nightmare. When things could not worsen any further, Mr. Malhotra opted out leaving Dr. Singh deep in debt and with no choice but to take up teaching at an agriculture university near Nainital. This would, in some measure, help meet his own and his son's growing financial needs. The kothi occupied by Mr. Malhotra and the workshop was rented out to supplement the income.

As Vivek left the teens behind he became more sober. He now missed the warm and comforting presence of his mother and Baba and realised that in his pursuit of joys he had failed to see their sorrow. He cursed himself for a cad and an ungrateful wretch. It dawned on him that no one else's grandfather had done as much as his Baba. He now missed even the earthy wisdom of his words of advice. As he looked into the face of the portrait in the living room his heart ached. There would be no Baba to share in his joy and to bless him.

Around noon, the doorbell rang. The khansama came to inform Vivek that a lawyer was there to see him. Vivek's first thought was, "Maybe, the house is going to be auctioned to pay off Papa's debts, but then surely the lawyer would want to see Papa not me."

Seeing the worried look the lawyer put him at ease and congratulated him. He informed Vivek that his grandfather had set up a trust for him a few years back after selling the orchards and a few fields and had stipulated that from his twenty first birthday he would get one thousand rupees each month.

Tears came to Vivek's eyes. Clutching the cheque he ran to the living room and standing before the portrait murmured, **"Thank you Baba for this very welcome gift. I had wished you were here and you are!"**

8

Would she really want to know?

The three girls were like the primary colours. Each was different and yet blended into a harmonious collage. Vineeta was serene and sensitive and always ready with help and sincere advice. Kiran's sunny disposition and matching radiant smile turned grumpy grouches into smileys. Lavanya was the red-hot chilli full of oomph and brimming with zest for life. She believed in no holds barred.

The first day at college has a strange way of throwing together very disparate elements and thus it was that these three became friends for life. Friends share rooms, books, food, clothes and secrets. These even had a common love interest! Prahlad was the handsomest hunk in college and unwittingly, all three fell for his charms. He, like Krisna of the Maharaas, made each of the three girls feel special. Soon, however, Vineeta realized that Prahlad could never be more than 'just a good friend' and dropped out of the competition leaving the field clear for Kiran and Lavanya. The pendulum swung merrily. Each girl had her array of weapons. It was going to be a close race but those who knew Lavanya were prepared to stake their last rupee on her. Her pout was becoming sexier, her voice huskier and her dresses shorter. The cheer leaders of the Lavanya camp had just set the champagne to chill when they got the heart breaking news—Prahlad had proposed to Kiran and she had accepted. They were amazed. How would Lavanya take it? Lavnya took it sportingly and congratulated Prahlad and Kiran who had decided to get married that same winter.

Then came the bombshell. Lavanya was getting married on Ram Navmi a month before Prahlad and Kiran. More amazingly, it was an arranged marriage. Her friends were sure a hurt heart had affected her head! Most had no grouse against Kiran and thought the competition had been stiff but fair, but…The wedding was a low-key affair and the friends did not get to share in the fun they had been looking forward to all this while. Lavanya went away to Singapore with her husband. She did not attend Kiran's wedding.

The three girls maintained contact and exchanged family photographs over the net

Now at last after three years they were to be together. They were going to spend a whole week together at Kiran's apartment and share in the joy of the birth of her first baby. Unfortunately, their husbands would not accompany Vineeta and Lavanya. Never mind, it would be like old times!

Quite a crowd had come for the celebrations and Kiran was very apologetic she could not offer her dearest friends separate bedrooms. "Never mind, Kiran, we have come here to share in your joy not to sleep!" chided Vineeta. She had got married only a few weeks back and was enjoying herself. She had always loved children and this was her special friend's baby. She helped with the changing of diapers and went about with a smile, probably thinking of the time when she herself would be a mother.

The week slipped by quickly. This was the last night of their stay. Vineeta was going through the memories of her honeymoon and thinking about her husband. Deepak might not be very handsome but he was a nice person, warm and caring. She had just started to doze off when she heard stealthy footfalls. Who could it be this time of night? She opened her eyes and in the faint glow of the night lamp she saw a shadow bent over Lavanya. To her horror she realized it was Prahlad.

"Do you want something, Prahlad?" Vineeta asked hoping that would send the message that she was awake and he should leave.

The strangely bitter voice of Lavanya sliced the atmosphere. "What he wants, I will give, you go to sleep!"

Vineeta was filled with revulsion. Sleep, she was too ashamed to be in the same room with this slut. She gathered her nightgown close to herself and left the room sobbing softly. Now what? Blind with sorrow and anger she crossed the dining room and made for Kiran's room. Both mother and baby were sleeping peacefully. She did not know what to do or say. The whole thing was abominable. The serenity on Kiran's face was unbearable. How could she sleep peacefully when her world was about to be desecrated? Vineeta flopped down on the bed beside her friend. She wanted to reach out and put a soothing hand on her friend's shoulder but was afraid of awakening her. What would she say if Kiran asked what was troubling her? She had to first disentangle her own emotions if she was to be of any use to her friend. Even as she was contemplating the course of action, Kiran's hand reached out for hers but she did not say a word. Maybe a sincere touch can do more than well thought out words. Soon both women were asleep.

Even a dark night has its dawn and so did this. Next day Vineeta and Lavanya took leave. Kiran did not press them to stay on. "I know you have had an uncomfortable night; we will meet again some other time!" she said.

Life went on as before for Kiran and Prahlad. She did not ask where he had gone off to in the middle of the night and he did not have to resort to subterfuge. Kiran did not say anything about Vineeta either.

Today, more than a decade later, that night has come back to haunt Vineeta. Her sister, Sulbha, has been staying with her. She is more like a daughter as there is a lot of difference in their ages. She loves her tenderly and watches over her like a tigress. This often leads to heated arguments with her husband. This morning Deepak was very angry. Sulbha's door was bolted from the inside and he needed to take out his jacket from the wardrobe. This has happened twice before. Vineeta is intrigued as this has been a recent practice. Sulbha never bothered to close the door even in the night earlier. Ordinarily she would have asked her sister about it but this time she is not sure she wants to really know the reason for this strange behavior. She has observed Sulbha deliberately distance herself from her brother-in-law. Vineeta's womanly instincts tell her Sulbha has some solid justification. Her thoughts go back to that dark night. Did Kiran too suspect the worst that night and did not want to confront the truth because she did not feel up to it just as she does now? A fool's paradise is still a paradise; some truths are better left buried. Vineeta does not have the courage to probe into the truth. She wants to believe Deepak is still the loving, caring husband he has always been with eyes only for her. Besides, her sister may not tell her the truth for fear of hurting her. **Kiran had not wanted to know that night; Vineeta does not want to know today.**

9

God be her guardian angel

It was a stag party very like any other but for the small detail…Mahipal was getting married a week later. The bonhomie that accelerated with each passing peg soon obliterated the fine line that separates right from wrong. Soon, horns blaring and car speakers screaming, the party was wending its way to a posh-looking house with a picture-postcard setting.

It was all Ravi's idea and Ravi could do no wrong. His friends were always a little in awe of him. He had done God proud by working on the good looks he had been endowed with! His father often enthused, "Sadda Ravi to hira hai!" and hardly a soul disagreed. Amit joked that Ravi had left the Raymond Complete Man out in the cold. Over and above his handsome looks and charismatic personality, Ravi had a mansion to love in, a retinue of servants at his beck and call, an imported car, a cushy job, supportive parents, a wonderful wife…sweet, beautiful and doting and girls galore. Mahipal, coming from a conservative family, was shy and awkward with the opposite sex. Even when he had gone to see Anjana, he had sat there tongue-tied and transfixed and Anjana, secretly charmed by this silly 'goochie poochie', had taken the initiative and 'interviewed' him. Ravi had chuckled when he heard the story and, though Mahipal was not told, this visit was part of the remedial action at making him 'more of a man'.

Ravi seemed to be very popular at this house. Uncleji and Auntieji received the party with open arms and introduced their four young and beautiful daughters. A lazy thought drifted into Mahipal's mind. It's not going to be easy to find husbands for so many daughters, even as comely as these. This must be one amorous family to have produced a quartet even as the government is crying itself hoarse preaching, 'hum do hamare do'. God bless them!

During the chai nashta, equations fell into place and Mahipal found himself ensconced in a sofa with a winsome girl his own age. Preeti, for that was her name, took his hand and looking deep into his eyes murmured, "To chalein."

So engrossed had Mahipal been in his discussion on the advantages of living in South Delhi with Uncleji that he hadn't noted that the others, including Auntieji, had left the room. Atthe door of Preeti's room, the hard reality hit him. "Oh my God, this is a whore house!" These are not daughters lined up by parents eager to beget a boy child but call girls with a pimp and a madam keeping a close eye on the cash register. Better sense should have prevailed but didn't. The liquor had addled his brains. Moreover, fear of derision by peer group engenders a feeling of bravado. Soon, Mahipal found himself enjoying the frenetic activity that followed.

There was a positive thing to say for this liaison. Mahipal was an experienced man when he lifted the veil off his bride's pretty face on the suhaag raat.

Days rushed by as they do on an extended honeymoon. Life was one whirlwind of job responsibilities and a new bride. There was little time for socializing. Friends cribbed that Mahipal had become a joroo ka ghulaam but they understood.

Meanwhile, of late, Ravi had not been his effervescent self. He tired easily and seemed to have become the favourite target of each passing virus. His resilience too was decreasing. Worried parents and friends told him to consult a doctor but Ravi told them not to worry. It was a bit of a nuisance which would soon pass.

That was not to be. For the next five months Ravi was in and out of hospitals. There was something very wrong with him which doctors either hadn't diagnosed or were unwilling to divulge. Meanwhile, Ravi was losing weight fast and his complexion was turning a sickly grey. The first three months had not been so bad. In between hospital visits, Ravi had been able to put in an appearance at the office. Now, even when he seemed well, he felt too tired and weak to get out of bed for anything but the call of nature. At the outset, the family had tried a few private clinics but soon Ravi switched over to a government hospital. Friends tried to cheer him up and once in a while their wives accompanied them. While Ravi perked up with these visits, his wife, Namrata, remained dejected and morose. She seemed enveloped in an aura of inevitability.

Another six months crawled by. For Ravi it was a journey down an abyss of pain and growing despair. He realised that the end was near.

Eleven o'clock in the night is not a good time for a telephone to ring a newly-wed friend. The ringing became persistent and almost screamed for attention. Reluctantly, Mahipal reached for the phone.In response to his curt "Hello" there was uncontrollable sobbing at the other end. An unnamed fear got hold of Mahipal. He looked in the direction of the puja room and sent up a silent prayer for his friend. He tried to calm down Ravi's wife. When, finally, Namrata could speak intelligibly, Mahipal understood that Ravi was critically ill and wanted to see his friends. Mahipal got the necessary details and shakily put the phone down. He turned his ashen face towards Anjana and in a cracking whisper said, "We have to go and see Ravi immediately. He is very sick."

The time for love-making was over. The claims of friendship must prevail. This moment would be the beginning of a torturous rollercoaster ride for all concerned.

The handful of friends Ravi had sent an urgent message to had turned up. In little ways they were trying to make him comfortable. Avinash tried to lighten the melancholy by cracking some weak jokes but Ravi cut in. "I have AIDS," he said in an almost inaudible whisper.

If a bomb had been dropped, it could not have made a greater impact

The chilling silence was broken by an avalanche of responses to soothe the nerves oftheir dying friend. Then, as if on cue they fell quiet once again, perhaps waiting for Ravi to elaborate or, more likely, because by now the true portent had sunk in. The next sentence skewered into each heart. An unnamed dread was taking a form. Ravi said, "I called all of you especially as you too might be at ris. Remember that brothel we went to before Mahip's wedding...Well I had been a regular there for some years…two of the girls, Preeti and Bani died recently...I am sorry I took you there. Now I am paying with my life."

Each word was like a poisoned dart right on target. Panic took the place of concern. So far they had been spectators not actors in the tragedy. Now they were not sure of their status. In their minds they cursed this 'satan incarnate' forgetting they had been willing followers with brains they could have used had they wanted to. Self-inflicted wounds hurt the most so it is easier to blame others for one's ordeals. Without a word or a handshake the company departed one by one leaving Ravi to the tomb-like iciness of his room. A week later Ravi died. Not a friend from this group turned up to lend a shoulder to the bier. Each reasoned that they would be more use to his family and being at the funeral was a mere formality. Actually they were scared that the virus would affect them. Dread and a sense of guilt of betrayal kept them from going to Ravi's home ever again.

For our protagonist, Mahipal, the next few days went by in deliberate dithering. Ignorance is truly bliss and for most of us a fool's paradise is the only one we will ever have. He reasoned that one thoughtless fling was all he was guilty of, unlike Ravi.

However, as a precautionary measure he decided not to have sex until the little matter had been cleared. This was not easy. Anjana had no inkling of his premarital dalliance and it would be unfair to burden her with unproven fears. Maybe if all turned out well she need never be told of the unfortunate incident. Mahipal loved his wife very much and wanted to protect her from any sort of hurt or unhappiness.

The urgency to get the check-up done came in an very way. That day Anjana coyly handed Mahipal a shopping list. At the top of it were six balls of baby wool. And, it had been underlined. Never have eyes so sparkled with joy for so fleeting a moment. Mahipal drew his wife into a strong embrace and smothered her with kisses but there was something amiss. There was too much tenderness and not enough youthful exuberance.

Mahipal chose the government hospital farthest away from his home. He hoped to get a clean chit but a little precaution would do no harm. The cruel treatment friends had meted out to Ravi was still fresh in his mind.

Then, horror struck. The very first report blew all wishful thinking to the winds and Mahipal's dreams came crashing down. He had tested HIV positive. True, the doctor tried to play down the whole thing and reassured him that he had several healthful years provided he led a safe life style and took care of his general health. AIDS was not an imminent sceptre. Meanwhile, he should enjoy life. To Mahipal, however, it seemed as if the death warrant had been signed. Now he should begin to count the days and pray for a reasonably pain-free end. Mahipal could not decide if he should be grateful that Ravi had let them in on the horrible truth or curse him for taking away his peace of mind for as yet he had not yet manifested any signs of the dread disease.

The immediate problem was breaking the news to his family, especially Anjana. He decided to keep the most difficult task for the last. This turned out to be the right strategy. The first reaction of his parents was totally unwarranted. “That shameless slut must have had an affair and now my poor innocent boy will suffer,” spat his mother, eyes filled with deep hate. Mahipal had to rush to his wife’s defence. He explained the events that led to his misfortune. They couldn’t believe their son was the villain but had to hold their horses. Mahipal made them promise they would treat Anjana with sensitivity as she was a victim of their son’s wrongdoing.

Mahipal had been somewhat prepared but for Anjana it would come as a rude shock. The dreams they had shared would now be tinged with shades of grey. He was filled with anguish and remorse at what he had led his unsuspecting wife into. The doctor had warned that his wife too may be at risk and suggested that Mahipal should minimise the damage by practising safe sex henceforth. As and when she showed any signs of weight loss, low grade fever over time or diarrhoea she should be tested also. Mahipal prayed to God that in his infinite mercy He would spare Anjana or if that were too much to hope for, at least grant them a few healthy years in which they could see the child lisp, toddle and with a bit of luck, even get through primary school. Beyond that he dared not look in case he tempted fate.

The fact that Anjana was pregnant came in useful. Mahipal played a doting yet anxious husband. Physical love gave way to tender loving care. Anjana was on cloud nine. Mahipal decided to wait till after the birth of the baby. If all was well he would pick courage and take Anjana and the baby for check up.

The birth of the baby girl brought a lot of cheer. Mahipal wanted to savour each moment of her growing up. She was a rosy-cheeked little cherub and that gave Mahipal a lot of satisfaction. However, the little canker in his mind was working full-time and each time Anjana started to weave dreams for the future, Mahipal’s heart would quail and he would cross his fingers.

The little one was about two months old and soon it was time to resume love-making. This was also the time Mahipal would have to divulge the horrible secret.

In the stillness of the jasmine-scented night, as the two lay entwined, Mahipal took Anjana’s hand in his and said softly, “Anju, I have

something terrible to tell you. I have tested HIV positive. And, oh my love, I may have even passed on the disease to you."

Anjana sat up in bed. All she could utter was, "Oh God!" She neither asked him how he came by it nor how he could have been so cruel to her whom he loved so much. Her only thought was for their child, the apple of their eyes, so tiny and helpless. She snatched up the little one from its cradle and wailed, "Mahip, what will happen to our baby now? What if I too test positive?"

The next thought made her embrace her child as if for the last time and quickly put it back in the cradle. "Oh my little darling, maybe your own mother will be your greatest enemy. O God, please look after her and keep her from all harm." She then turned to Mahipal and said, "From tomorrow I will come into contact with her as little as possible and her dadiji can feed her off a bottle. Thank God she has a grandmother who cherishes her!"

Mahipal laid aside his own fears and was now a pillar of strength. He told her there was no immediate danger according to the doctor. He had asked the doctor about the breast feeding of the babe and now said encouragingly, "You are the best for our baby and on your milk she will thrive. You and my mother will do a great job."

The two lay talking throughout the tortuous night discussing what measures to take. The next day Anjana too would see the doctor. Whatever the news, they would face life together and do their best by the baby so that she lacked nothing.

Anjana's tests confirmed what they had feared. However, there was a redeeming factor. Both were still in the early stages of the disease so they could go about their daily duties for some years yet. Daily, new research was helping contain the dreadful aspects allowing a more full life. In a way, things had turned out reasonably well. Regular counselling coupled with sensible living would extend their life and they could take necessary measures to lay by some money for the child. The baby is seven months old and has had all her inoculations as per schedule. She looks well but to be on the safe side, she has been tested for HIV infection. She has cleared the first test but to be doubly sure, the doctor wanted a second test done. Anjana is overcome by all her earlier anxieties but Mahipal has steeled himself and decided to face the situation in a positive manner. The results of the second test are due today.

The past two weeks had seemed endless but now Time seems to have stopped moving. There are two patients ahead of them. The first patient goes in. Minutes tick by. The suspense in the waiting room is just beginning to get oppressive when the next person is called in. Now it will be their turn. The baby squirms in Anjana's arms. She clutches her even more tightly. Mahipal reaches out to hold his wife's clammy hand. Neither speaks but the glances they exchange mirror their anxiety. Every minute seems like an era.

"Next!"

Anjana and Mahipal close their eyes in silent prayer, "God, please be with our little one!"

The doctor greets Anjana and Mahipal with a cheery smile and says, "You are a very fortunate couple, your baby has tested negative!"

God has been merciful. The baby is safe. Floodgates burst open and Anjana lets out a little sob of relief, "O God, thank you! Please be her Guardian Angel!"

10

Written in the stars

The incessant drone of the Mahamritunjaya jaap hangs like a pall over the neighbourhood. The tones are emerging from Pandit Kalicharan's house. Yama, the God of Death, is expected to pay a call any time today. As everyone knows, the chanting of the mantra has the power to ward off death or make it easy.

Strangely, to the casual onlooker, there does not seem to be anyone in imminent danger of dying. The mood of the gathered crowd too is more hopefully expectant than gloomy. Pandit Kalichran is an astrologer, numerologist and palm reader of some eminence. So far most, nay, almost all, his predictions have come true so how can this go wrong. There is not a sliver of doubt in his mind. Today is the day.

A rumour can metamorphose into an exciting scoop and with so many 24-hour news channels in the fray every little story counts. This one has all the high drama of a human-interest story. Since early morning reporters have been descending on this remote village of Uttar Pradesh. Ever wondered how these reporters get to a scene so fast? Their long noses can smell a story or their compass needles point not to the North but to any place that promises an interesting tale. The needle quivers urgently indicating they are warm as they draw up close and sits motionless like Mr. Clippit when they veer away.

All angles have been thrashed out by now and opinion polls taken. Now the reporters sit at a decent distance from the cynosure and anxiously watch out for any tell tale signs of pre-death discomfort. Such scenes are common in hospitals where loving relatives eye each flicker on the monitor with hope or despair. The reporters have the advantage of detachment.

Krishna Bhatia, the newcomer, is obviously a novice. He looks around tentatively and then approaches the charpoy on which Kalicharan is seated in noble splendour, large turban et al. "I've heard someone from this village has predicted his own death for today. Can I see him?"

He might just as well have lobbed a hand grenade at the crowd. For a second all forget to breathe and then there is commotion.

"The insensitive, insolent twerp," a village elder bellows.

Krishna realises he has made a faux pas and starts to blubber out apologies, "I'm extremely sorry. I…"

Another reporter tries to soothe ruffled feathers. "Arre Baba, there is no need to get so agitated. Most of us here are unable to believe Panditji will soon be no more. He looks as healthy as anyone else!"

"You city folk!" another villager spits contemptuously.

Krishna realises that no fellow news reporter is going to help. His eyes light up when he sees a policeman. Surely, he would be of help and if duly impressed, he might even help him get a ringside seat!

"Darogaji, I've heard that the most eminent astrologer in this area has prophesied his own death. Do you know who he is and where I can find him? I am from the Kal ka Samachar," he adds for good measure, "and your contribution will find due place in the story!"

The policeman disinterestedly points in the direction of Pandit Kalicharan's charpoy by now almost hidden from view by a swarm of reporters all of whom had tried to win him over similarly!

An elderly woman dressed in bridal finery, complete with mangal tika and red bangles emerges from Panditji's doorway and sits beside Panditji who tenderly pats her hand. She is very quietly for sometime and then goes back inside. The rituals for Karva Chauth are time-consuming and this time she has to be extra careful.

One of the villagers voices the collective thoughts of the entire community, "It's unfortunate Yama has chosen this day, Panditji's wife is a pativrataas the whole village knows and her whole life revolves round Panditji !"

"She will be totally devastated," put in Parvati, Panditji's immediate neighbour.

"All I know about rituals, I have learnt from Panditayan."

"It's unfortunate Yama has chosen this day, Panditji's wife is a pativrata as the whole village knows and her whole life revolves round Panditji. She will be totally devastated," put in Parvati, Panditji's immediate neighbour.

"You know, all I know about rituals I have learnt from Panditayan," says a young woman feelingly."

The focus of interest has turned away from Panditji towards his wife whose emotions are running the full gamut of hope and despair. Each year she has observed the Karva chauth fast and prayed earnestly for the long life of her husband and beseeched Gaura maiya to ensure she dies a suhagan. It is a tussle between her belief that the Mother Goddess will not abandon her to such a terrible fate and her awareness of Panditji's vast sea of knowledge that has forecast widowhood for her. Can she dare hope that this once he might have erred in his calculations. She goes through the motions of the rituals performed for the last fifty one years, mechanically.

Panditji passed on the ominous bit of information only a week ago hoping to minimise the duration of trauma and yet give his wife time enough to prepare herself though in his mind and heart he knows that no woman is ever prepared for such an eventuality. As expected, she did not believe him at first. The words were spoken very gently as Panditji held her hand tenderly. She stared in horror. Panditji was not given to jesting and this was hardly amusing. As the portent seeped in a muffled sob caught in her throat.

Each year this had been a day of happy celebration and like every wife, young or old she had decked herself in her wedding lehnga, applied alta on her feet and henna on her hands. Painstakingly she would smear the portion of the kitchen wall reserved for the motifs for puja on Karva Chauth. The second portion was reserved for Diwali. The mud for the Gaura idol she brought from the riverbed so it was really clean. The special sweets were made in a large quantity as Panditji really appreciated her cooking. Advancing years had not numbed her enthusiasm and she looked forward to the fasting not with dread but with joy. Their compatible natures were a source of admiration and the tenderness between them had only grown with the years.

Ramgarh is the regional hub and there is a yearly mela beginning just after Dusshera and culminating the day after Karva Chauth. Families come by bullockcart, tractor, jalopies and buses from nearby villages. The Ramlila maidan's kiosks, large and small, are chock-a-block with colourful bangles, lehngas, karvas, mehndi, Karva Chauth charts and mulit-coloured bindis. Now is the time to indulge. Firozabad sends reshmi and katav bangles, which have a pleasant jingle, are in high demand. Red is the colour of the season but bangles of all colours are stocked up for the year. Also they make lovely presents. The lacquer kangans from Jaipur are equally popular. They are embellished with beads and bits of mirror which sparkle in the sun! The so called ivory churas are acyually made of plastic but are, nonetheless, popular among young Punjabi brides. The silversmith stalls are stocked with bichiyas and payals in a variety of designs old and new. These are important accessories of this festival and the demand is high.

Even though prices are rocketing sky high, this is no time for such petty considerations and while older women prefer their wedding outfits, young women buy new lehnga cholis. Their husbands indulge them. After all the wife is doing it all for the longevity of the husband's life!

There are shops selling puja essentials. Pictorial depictions of the brother showing the supposed moon through a sieve to his younger sister standing on top of a banyan tree are a must for young brides unwilling to go through the tedium of depicting the same on their kitchen walls. The influence of TV serials has spilled over into real life; sieves and mehndi sell like hot cakes. Young girls and a few boys have learnt the art of applying mehndi and make tidy income.

The main story seems to have gone into slumber mode. Luckily, a rumour has gained ground that a film is being shot in a nearby village. The crowd of journalists starts to thin. Might just as well cover the shooting for now and come back later to see how Panditji is faring. It is, anyway, hardly very sensitive looking at one's watch every now and then, ears open for the mournful wail connoting his departure to the soul to the world beyond.

Left alone, Pandit Kalicharan got busy with his ritual prayers. He had called his childhood friend, Pandit Lakshmi Das, to be on hand to perform his last rites when the time came. The latter suggested that gau daan would help in the process of smooth salvation. A young milch cow was brought. No hanky panky here. Usually an old cow is made do with but here Pandit Lakshmi Das would be the beneficiary! Mantras are read and Pandit Kalicharan is made to hold the tail of the cow that has been reverently been applied tilak to. The belief is that the soul will rise to heaven holding the cow's tail.

Meanwhile, Panditayan has been carrying on with the preparations for the puja. The pious ardour is accompanied with an unnamed uneasiness.

Hope and dread sit side by side in a roller coaster of emotions. The motifs on the kitchen wall are testimony of her trembling hands. Everything has taken a lot more time. She has been extra careful lest some little detail gets left out bringing the wrath of the deities upon her. This is the first time she has asked a friend to give a final look over! By and by the chauk is made, Gaura placed in the centre, the special delicacies fried and karvas for herself and Gaura filled with water. There is feverishness in the performance of the rituals. At last it is time for moonrise. A shout goes up from the little boys and girls, "Chaand nikal aaya!"

Finishing touches are given to the pujas, karvas exchanged with Gaura and each suhaagan emerges from her doorway with her karva behind her sari pallav to offering argh to the moon.

A team of journalists has come back. One wise guy asks Panditayan. "Kaisa lag raha hai?"

The ear to ear smile says it all but her heart has put celebrations on hold. A few more hours then all will be right with her world.

After the hectic day the journalists decide to leave for the night. Panditayan who has not taken a drop of water the whole day takes a happy sip from the water in the karva offered by her husband. Gratefully, they eat their food with frequent loving glances and smiles. Panditji is coaxed into lying down and is soon snoring softly. Panditain sitting by his bed too dozes off.

From the next day, equations change in the village. Panditayan's piousness has driven away Yama, has it not? She is Gaura's anointed one! Women throng to her door to seek her blessings. Panditji's renown as fortune teller may have taken a beating somewhat but Panditain's cash registers have more than made up for it. He is not complaining! He is more than grateful to God for giving him such a devoted wife whose piety has snatched him from the clutches of death just as Satyavan had been reclaimed by his wife, Savitri!

11

How could you, papa?

It was a day like any other but that day I lost everything. Sonia, my best friend had gone to buy bread for breakfast. When she did not return even after an hour, Suman Aunty rang up Gupta Stores. Sonia had not gone there. Where was she? She rang me up next but though we met every day it was only after five o'clock. It was now that Aunty started to worry. All the children of the colony were amazed. Where could Sonia have gone so early in the morning? It was decided that before getting police help we should conduct a thorough search on our own. All day the search went on but we couldn't find Sonia. The police had to be called. We kids took the police to all our favourite secret places but she was nowhere to be found. The police brought two dogs. After sometime the dogs started to bark loudly; they had found something. It was Sonia's tiny body hidden among the bushes in our park. We play hide and seek in the park but never go to that corner. It is dark and scary and very smelly. How did Sonia get there?

The area was cordoned off and the policemen set about looking for anything that would help them get to the culprit. The child lay in a crumpled heap. She was hardly seven years old but had put up a valiant fight. Pieces of the colourful bangles, the tinkling music of which she loved so much, lay all over the place.

Sonia's parents, grandparents and elder brother wailed uncontrollably. Sonia was gone forever. Her innocent chatter would no longer warm their hearts. The cute smile and twinkling eyes would be a haunting memory.

She looked like a bashed doll. The lovely pink polka frock her brother gave her for rakhi was torn and muddy. We had exchanged friendship bands just as our dollies had! Her tightly clutched fist held something. Her face was streaked with dust which had settled on the tears streaming down her face. It was horrible. How she must have cried for mercy. The crushed marigold plants seemed to be sobbing. How could anyone be so cruel to a sweet little girl like Sonia? Surely the person must have a very evil mind.

I clutched my father's hand in a tight grip and said "You know, Papa, Sonia's dolly is just like the doll teacher uses to teach us about good and bad touch and when our teacher asked what we would do if someone touched us in a bad way, Sonia used to shout 'help, help' the loudest. Poor thing she couldn't even cry out aloud as police uncle says her mouth was full of chocolate. This is very strange as teacher says we must not accept food from strangers! Do only strangers do bad things? Do you think Sonia knew the person? Police says they are sure Sonia knew the person."

"It is better not to take anything from anyone," Papa said and put his arm protectively round me.

I was agitated and went on, "Some bad uncle must have kidnapped and killed her, isn't it, Papa?" He did not say anything but clutched me close to his heart.

The next four days were bad, really bad. It was like a stormy night with no dawn in sight. Everyone seemed gloomy or grumpy. Smiles had disappeared from 'Ashiana', our colony, known for its serenity and feeling of security, where children could be seen playing badminton even at midnight! People kept to themselves and did not venture out much. I went to Sonia's place but did not know what to say and started to weep.

Every day Sonia's father, Deepak uncle, went to the police station to find out what progress, if any, the police had made. Papa accompanied him. Deepak uncle was grateful for this.

On the fifth day papa was asked to report at the police station. This made little sense. Mummy was furious. "See what you've got yourself into with your Samaritan nature! Now you will do rounds of the courts as if you are the only witness!"

Papa did not return that day or the next. I felt uneasy, had the police arrested him?

In the colony, all hell broke loose.

"The villain lived amongst us and we had no idea!"

"I can still not believe it, there must be some mistake."

"He is very close to his own daughter and loved the children and was a great favourite with them."

"How will the kids react when they hear this?"

"The older ones will be horrified and the little ones will not understand. Either way it is bad."

"His family is so nice, how are they going to face this?"

"And to think the two families are so close!"

"It is unfair on the two lovable kids! They will be asked all sorts of uncomfortable questions!"

"If it was murder of an adult one could understand, but murder of an innocent child!"

No one saw me but I heard all this and it made no sense. Were they talking about my papa?

This was not the same Ashiana where everyone laughed and talked all the time. I and my family were no more welcome at other houses.

People tried to soothe Deepak uncle and Suman auntie. I too had lost my dearest friend but there was only pity in the eyes of the Ashiana residents and it was unbearable . Nobody talked to us. Our whole family was somehow tarnished. No one visited the us anymore. Vikrant bhayia was the hero of the cricket team . He was a good wicket keeper and had played a major role in winning matches against the neighbouring colony. Now it seemed there was no place for him either in the hearts of his friends or in the team. This is not fair. What have we done for which we are being punished? Mummy frequently hugs us but she is sad all the time. The hug does not take my pain away. I have become very quiet and depressed and weep at almost anything. My brother, Vikrant, has become abusive and violent. His friends tease him mercilessly. He has become overly protective towards me as he is worried about me. I am not sent to run errands anymore. Suddenly the world has become very unsafe! Strangely, Papa has just vanished. Where is Papa? He has never been away so long on a tour. Previously he rang up every day and talked to me the longest. I miss him so much but bhaiya gets all nettled when I ask about him.

Ultimately, school reopens but things are no better here. Even my classmates don't like to talk to me. They maliciously whisper words like 'killer' and 'rapist' and look slyly in my direction. It is horrible.

By now I know Papa has killed Sonia and everyone hates us for that but I do not know the meaning of 'rapist'. Back home, I ask Mummy what it means She tries to put me off. I insist. She weeps and weeps and hugs me tight and whispers, "It is bad touch." I am shocked. I am reminded of the sweet little doll and the lesson in good and bad touch. "The person who touches in a bad way is bad." Does that mean Papa is bad? I have always thought my father is the best and love him a lot and cannot believe this at first. Bhaiya silently nods when I ask if what Mummy has told me is true. My heart cries out, "How could you, Papa? Sonia was my best friend and you called her 'beti' just as you call me. Then, how could you do such a bad thing to her? I am ashamed of you!'

Mummy has taken up a job as receptionist at an office. Maybe she is bored and lonely. My grandparents have come to stay with us. Baba helps us with our studies and reads us stories. He goes to the market when we need anything. He loves us a lot but I still miss Papa. Dadi cooks the lunch and Mummy makes dinner. Dadi goes to the weekly puja in the colony. Now that is our only connection with Ashiana.

We will be moving out soon. Baba says we cannot afford the big house anymore but I overheard some uncles saying that our landlord has asked us to vacate the house. Where will we go? I am scared. I was born here. I didn't even know this house was rented.

Baba tells me we were not only leaving the colony but also this city. We will now move to Raipur where my Chacha lives. I am happy, at least my cousins, Arpita and Mohit will be there. We will not live with them but can at least celebrate festivals together!

The change in scene has been beneficial. Slowly but surely life has come back on track. We have started to enjoy the little things of life and to appreciate them! We smile and laugh. Bhaiya and I have made many new friends and Mummy has once again started hosting fabulous parties!

I am no more a little girl. I have just started college. Life has taught me a lot but the most important thing is that bad times come with an expiry date too. Sooner or later good times return and life goes on. The new place has been good for us. Bhaiya has finished his graduation. He studied hard and having got a scholarship is all set for an IT course. I am my old cheerful, confident self. I have seven close friends. We are known as the Rainbow Girls and help people in need. All of us have learnt self-defence techniques and happily teach them to all young girls in our vicinity. I know there are rapists but cannot put my life on hold. After all we have only one life and I believe that being a girl should not be a disadvantage. A girl can do all a boy can and more! Grant her space and security and watch her blossom!